Selected Stories by
RUDYARD KIPLING

Books in this Series:

Selected Stories by O. Henry

Selected Stories by Anton Chekhov

Selected Stories by Guy de Maupassant

Selected Stories by Mark Twain

Selected Stories by Edgar Allan Poe

Selected Stories by Rudyard Kipling

Selected Stories by Saki

Selected Stories by Oscar Wilde

Selected Stories by Honoré de Balzac

Selected Stories by Charles Dickens

Selected Stories by D.H. Lawrence

Selected Stories by H.G. Wells

Selected Stories by Jack London

Selected Stories by Joseph Conrad

Selected Stories by Leo Tolstoy

Selected Stories by Sir Arthur Conan Doyle

Selected Stories by
RUDYARD KIPLING

Published by
Rupa Publications India Pvt. Ltd 2014
7/16, Ansari Road, Daryaganj
New Delhi 110002

Sales Centres:
Allahabad Bengaluru Chennai
Hyderabad Jaipur Kathmandu
Kolkata Mumbai

Selection and Introduction copyright © Terry O'Brien 2014

All rights reserved.
No part of this publication may be reproduced, transmitted,
or stored in a retrieval system, in any form or by any means,
electronic, mechanical, photocopying, recording or otherwise,
without the prior permission of the publisher.

ISBN: 978-81-291-3136-2

First impression 2014

10 9 8 7 6 5 4 3 2 1

Printed at Shree Maitrey Printech Pvt. Ltd., Noida

This book is sold subject to the condition that it shall not,
by way of trade or otherwise, be lent, resold, hired out, or otherwise
circulated, without the publisher's prior consent, in any form of binding or
cover other than that in which it is published.

CONTENTS

Introduction vii

1. The Elephant's Child ... 1
2. Rikki-Tikki-Tavi ... 10
3. How the Leopard got His Spots ... 27
4. Bread Upon the Waters ... 34
5. The Finest Story in the World ... 62
6. My Son's Wife ... 88
7. The City of Dreadful Night ... 124
8. Swept and Garnished ... 131

INTRODUCTION

Joseph Rudyard Kipling (30 December 1865–18 January 1936) was an English short-story writer, poet and novelist. He is remembered for his tales and poems about British soldiers in India, and his tales for children. He received the Nobel Prize for Literature in 1907.

Rudyard Kipling was born in Bombay, but educated in England at the United Services College, Westward Ho, Bideford. Kipling was born at the height of the British Raj, and so was brought up by Indian nurses (ayahs), who taught him something of the beliefs and tongues of India. In 1882, he returned to India, where he worked for Anglo-Indian newspapers. A prolific writer, he achieved fame quickly. In 1894 appeared his *The Jungle Book*, which became a children's classic all over the world. *Kim* (1901), the story of Kimball O'Hara and his adventures in the Himalayas, is perhaps his most felicitous work. Kipling was the recipient of many honorary degrees and other awards. In 1926 he received the Gold Medal of the Royal Society of Literature, which only Walter Scott, George Meredith and Thomas Hardy had been awarded before him.

- Read 'The Elephant's Child' to find out how, because of his insatiable curiosity, the elephant's child, and all the elephants thereafter, got long trunks.
- In 'Rikki-Tikki-Tavi', the brave mongoose Rikki-Tikki-Tavi matches himself in a legendary battle against the devilish

cobra Nag and his wife Nagina in the backyard of an English family's house in India.
- In 'How the Leopard got His Spots', all the animals are the same colour. The leopard is happy to be sandy-yellow and greyish-brown all over. But then Giraffe and Zebra go off to the forest and they begin to change. He goes to the specky-spicky-forest; and wonders if spots would be better.
- In 'Bread upon the Waters', McPhee, chief engineer of the shipping line of Holdock, Steiner & Chase is sacked, unreasonably, for refusing to fore his ship, the Breslan, to make timings she cannot keep.
- In 'The Finest Story in the World', the narrator meets a young bank clerk, Charlie, who longs to be a writer and seeks his advice. He produces powerful accounts of sea voyages in the ancient world, giving vivid details; the narrator becomes convinced that—rather than creating stories—he is remembering his past lives.
- 'My Son's Wife' is the story of the conversion of a town-dweller to the enduring virtues of English country life.
- In 'The City of Dreadful Night', racked by sleeplessness on an unusually hot night, the unnamed narrator chooses a random direction that takes him into the walled city.
- 'Swept and Garnished' is set in the autumn of 1914, in the early month of the Great War. Frau Ebermann has a touch of influenza. Hot and feverish, she takes to her bed while her maid makes her comfortable. Suddenly she sees a young child in the room and soon after, four more...

Rudyard Kipling is still the kind of author who can inspire passionate disagreement, and his place in literary and cultural history lives on.

1

THE ELEPHANT'S CHILD

In the High and Far-Off Times the Elephant, O Best Beloved, had no trunk. He had only a blackish, bulgy nose, as big as a boot, that he could wriggle about from side to side; but he couldn't pick up things with it. But there was one Elephant—a new Elephant—an Elephant's Child—who was full of 'satiable curtiosity, and that means he asked ever so many questions. *And* he lived in Africa, and he filled all Africa with his 'satiable curtiosities. He asked his tall aunt, the Ostrich, why her tail feathers grew just so, and his tall aunt, the Ostrich, spanked him with her hard, hard claw. He asked his tall uncle, the Giraffe, what made his skin spotty, and his tall uncle, the Giraffe, spanked him with his hard, hard hoof. And still he was full of 'satiable curtiosity! He asked his broad aunt, the Hippopotamus, why her eyes were red, and his broad aunt, the Hippopotamus, spanked him with her broad, broad hoof; and he asked his hairy uncle, the Baboon, why melons tasted just so, and his hairy uncle, the Baboon, spanked him with his hairy, hairy paw. And *still* he was full of 'satiable curtiosity! He asked questions about everything that he saw, or heard, or felt, or smelt, or touched, and all his uncles and his aunts spanked him. And still he was full of 'satiable curtiosity!

One fine morning in the middle of the Precession of the Equinoxes[1] this 'satiable Elephant's Child asked a new fine question that he had never asked before. He asked, 'What does the Crocodile have for dinner?' Then everybody said, 'Hush!' in a loud and dretful tone, and they spanked him immediately and directly, without stopping, for a long time.

By and by, when that was finished, he came upon Kolokolo Bird sitting in the middle of a wait-a-bit thorn-bush,[2] and he said, 'My father has spanked me, and my mother has spanked me; all my aunts and uncles have spanked me for my 'satiable curtiosity; and *still* I want to know what the Crocodile has for dinner!'

Then Kolokolo Bird said, with a mournful cry, 'Go to the banks of the great grey-green, greasy Limpopo River, all set about with fever trees,[3] and find out.'

That very next morning, when there was nothing left of the Equinoxes, because the Precession had preceded according to precedent, this 'satiable Elephant's Child took a hundred pounds of bananas (the little short red kind), and a hundred pounds of sugarcane (the long purple kind), and seventeen melons (the greeny-crackly kind), and said to all his dear families, 'Goodbye. I am going to the great grey-green, greasy Limpopo River, all set about with fever trees, to find out what the Crocodile has for dinner.' And they all spanked him once more for luck, though he asked them most politely to stop.

Then he went away, a little warm, but not at all astonished, eating melons, and throwing the rind about, because he could not pick it up.

He went from Graham's Town to Kimberley, and from Kimberley to Khama's Country,[4] and from Khama's Country he went east by north, eating melons all the time, till at last he came to the banks of the great grey-green, greasy Limpopo River, all set about with fever trees, precisely as Kolokolo Bird had said.

Now you must know and understand, O Best Beloved, that till that very week, and day, and hour, and minute, this 'satiable Elephant's Child had never seen a Crocodile, and did not know what one was like. It was all his 'satiable curtiosity.

The first thing that he found was a Bi-Coloured-Python-Rock-Snake curled round a rock.

''Scuse me,' said the Elephant's Child most politely, 'but have you seen such a thing as a Crocodile in these promiscuous parts?'

'*Have* I seen a Crocodile?' said the Bi-Coloured-Python-Rock-Snake, in a voice of dretful scorn. 'What will you ask me next?'

''Scuse me,' said the Elephant's Child, 'but could you kindly tell me what he has for dinner?'

Then the Bi-Coloured-Python-Rock-Snake uncoiled himself very quickly from the rock, and spanked the Elephant's Child with his scalesome, flailsome tail.

'That is odd,' said the Elephant's Child, 'because my father and my mother, and my uncle and my aunt, not to mention my other aunt, the Hippopotamus, and my other uncle, the Baboon, have all spanked me for my 'satiable curtiosity—and I suppose this is the same thing.'

So he said goodbye very politely to the Bi-Coloured-Python-Rock-Snake, and helped to coil him up on the rock again, and went on, a little warm, but not at all astonished, eating melons, and throwing the rind about, because he could not pick it up, till he trod on what he thought was a log of wood at the very edge of the great grey-green, greasy Limpopo River, all set about with fever trees.

But it was really the Crocodile, O Best Beloved, and the Crocodile winked one eye—like this!

''Scuse me,' said the Elephant's Child most politely, 'but do you happen to have seen a Crocodile in these promiscuous parts?'

Then the Crocodile winked the other eye, and lifted half his tail out of the mud; and the Elephant's Child stepped back most politely, because he did not wish to be spanked again.

'Come hither, Little One,' said the Crocodile. 'Why do you ask such things?'

''Scuse me,' said the Elephant's Child most politely, 'but my father has spanked me, my mother has spanked me, not to mention my tall aunt, the Ostrich, and my tall uncle, the Giraffe, who can kick ever so hard, as well as my broad aunt, the Hippopotamus, and my hairy uncle, the Baboon, *and* including the Bi-Coloured-Python-Rock-Snake, with the scalesome, flailsome tail, just up the bank, who spanks harder than any of them; and *so*, if it's quite all the same to you, I don't want to be spanked any more.'

'Come hither, Little One,' said the Crocodile, 'for I am the Crocodile,' and he wept crocodile-tears to show it was quite true.

Then the Elephant's Child grew all breathless, and panted, and kneeled down on the bank and said, 'You are the very person I have been looking for all these long days. Will you please tell me what you have for dinner?'

'Come hither, Little One,' said the Crocodile, 'and I'll whisper.'

Then the Elephant's Child put his head down close to the Crocodile's musky, tusky mouth, and the Crocodile caught him by his little nose, which up to that very week, day, hour, and minute, had been no bigger than a boot, though much more useful.

'I think,' said the Crocodile—and he said it between his teeth, like this—'I think today I will begin with Elephant's Child!'

At this, O Best Beloved, the Elephant's Child was much annoyed, and he said, speaking through his nose, like this, 'Led go! You are hurtig be!'

Then the Bi-Coloured-Python-Rock-Snake scuffled down from the bank and said, 'My young friend, if you do not now, immediately and instantly, pull as hard as ever you can, it is my opinion that your acquaintance in the large-pattern leather ulster' (and by this he meant the Crocodile) 'will jerk you into yonder limpid stream before you can say Jack Robinson.'

This is the way Bi-Coloured-Python-Rock-Snakes always talk.

Then the Elephant's Child sat back on his little haunches, and pulled, and pulled, and pulled, and his nose began to stretch. And the Crocodile floundered into the water, making it all creamy with great sweeps of his tail, and *he* pulled, and pulled, and pulled.

And the Elephant's Child's nose kept on stretching; and the Elephant's Child spread all his little four legs and pulled, and pulled, and pulled, and his nose kept on stretching; and the Crocodile threshed his tail like an oar, and *he* pulled, and pulled, and pulled, and at each pull the Elephant's Child's nose grew longer and longer—and it hurt him hijjus![5]

Then the Elephant's Child felt his legs slipping, and he said through his nose, which was now nearly five feet long, 'This is too butch for be!'

Then the Bi-Coloured-Python-Rock-Snake came down from the bank, and knotted himself in a double-clove-hitch[6] round the Elephant's Child's hind-legs, and said, 'Rash and inexperienced traveller, we will now seriously devote ourselves to a little high tension, because if we do not, it is my impression that yonder self-propelling man-of-war with the armour-plated upper deck' (and by this, O Best Beloved, he meant the Crocodile) 'will permanently vitiate your future career.'

That is the way all Bi-Coloured-Python-Rock-Snakes always talk.

So he pulled, and the Elephant's Child pulled, and the Crocodile pulled; but the Elephant's Child and the Bi-Coloured-Python-Rock-Snake pulled hardest; and at last the Crocodile let go of the Elephant's Child's nose with a plop that you could hear all up and down the Limpopo.

Then the Elephant's Child sat down most hard and sudden; but first he was careful to say 'Thank you' to the Bi-Coloured-Python-Rock-Snake; and next he was kind to his poor pulled nose, and wrapped it all up in cool banana leaves, and hung it in the great grey-green, greasy Limpopo to cool.

'What are you doing that for?' said the Bi-Coloured-Python-Rock-Snake.

''Scuse me,' said the Elephant's Child, 'but my nose is badly out of shape, and I am waiting for it to shrink.'

'Then you will have to wait a long time,' said the Bi-Coloured-Python-Rock-Snake. 'Some people do not know what is good for them.'

The Elephant's Child sat there for three days waiting for his nose to shrink. But it never grew any shorter, and, besides, it made him squint. For, O Best Beloved, you will see and understand that the Crocodile had pulled it out into a really truly trunk same as all Elephants have today.

At the end of the third day a fly came and stung him on the shoulder, and before he knew what he was doing he lifted up his trunk and hit that fly dead with the end of it.

''Vantage number one!' said the Bi-Coloured-Python-Rock-Snake. 'You couldn't have done that with a mere-smear nose. Try and eat a little now.'

Before he thought what he was doing the Elephant's Child put out his trunk and plucked a large bundle of grass, dusted it clean against his fore-legs, and stuffed it into his own mouth.

''Vantage number two!' said the Bi-Coloured-Python-Rock-Snake. 'You couldn't have done that with a mere-smear nose. Don't you think the sun is very hot here?'

'It is,' said the Elephant's Child, and before he thought what he was doing he schlooped up a schloop of mud from the banks of the great grey-green, greasy Limpopo, and slapped it on his head, where it made a cool schloopy-sloshy mud-cap all trickly behind his ears.

''Vantage number three!' said the Bi-Coloured-Python-Rock-Snake. 'You couldn't have done that with a mere-smear nose. Now how do you feel about being spanked again?'

''Scuse me,' said the Elephant's Child, 'but I should not like it at all.'

'How would you like to spank somebody?' said the Bi-Coloured-Python-Rock-Snake.

'I should like it very much indeed,' said the Elephant's Child.

'Well,' said the Bi-Coloured-Python-Rock-Snake, 'you will find that new nose of yours very useful to spank people with.'

'Thank you,' said the Elephant's Child, 'I'll remember that; and now I think I'll go home to all my dear families and try.'

So the Elephant's Child went home across Africa frisking and whisking his trunk. When he wanted fruit to eat he pulled fruit down from a tree, instead of waiting for it to fall as he used to do. When he wanted grass he plucked grass up from the ground, instead of going on his knees as he used to do. When the flies bit him he broke off the branch of a tree and used it as fly-whisk; and he made himself a new, cool, slushy-squshy mud-cap whenever the sun was hot. When he felt lonely walking through Africa he sang to himself down his trunk, and the noise was louder than several brass bands. He went specially out of his way to find a broad Hippopotamus (she was no relation of his), and he spanked her very hard, to make sure that the Bi-Coloured-Python-Rock-Snake had spoken the truth about his new trunk. The rest of the time he picked up the melon rinds that he had dropped on his way to the Limpopo—for he was a Tidy Pachyderm.[7]

One dark evening he came back to all his dear families, and he coiled up his trunk and said, 'How do you do?' They were very glad to see him, and immediately said, 'Come here and be spanked for your 'satiable curtiosity.'

'Pooh,' said the Elephant's Child. 'I don't think you peoples know anything about spanking; but *I* do, and I'll show you.'

Then he uncurled his trunk and knocked two of his dear brothers head over heels.

'O Bananas!' said they, 'where did you learn that trick, and what have you done to your nose?'

'I got a new one from the Crocodile on the banks of the great grey-green, greasy Limpopo River,' said the Elephant's Child. 'I asked him what he had for dinner, and he gave me this to keep.'

'It looks very ugly,' said his hairy uncle, the Baboon.

'It does,' said the Elephant's Child. 'But it's very useful,' and he picked up his hairy uncle, the Baboon, by one hairy leg, and hove him into a hornets' nest.

Then that bad Elephant's Child spanked all his dear families for a long time, till they were very warm and greatly astonished. He pulled out his tall Ostrich aunt's tail feathers; and he caught his tall uncle, the Giraffe, by the hind leg, and dragged him through a thorn bush; and he shouted at his broad aunt, the Hippopotamus, and blew bubbles into her ear when she was sleeping in the water after meals; but he never let anyone touch Kolokolo Bird.

At last things grew so exciting that his dear families went off one by one in a hurry to the banks of the great grey-green, greasy Limpopo River, all set about with fever trees, to borrow new noses from the Crocodile. When they came back nobody spanked anybody any more; and ever since that day, O Best Beloved, all the Elephants you will ever see, besides all those that you won't, have trunks precisely like the trunk of the 'satiable Elephant's Child.

I keep six honest serving-men
  (They taught me all I knew);
Their names are What and Why and When
  And How and Where and Who.
I send them over land and sea,
  I send them east and west;
But after they have worked for me,
  I give them all a rest.

I let them rest from nine till five,
   For I am busy then,
As well as breakfast, lunch, and tea,
   For they are hungry men:
But different folk have different views;
   I know a person small—
She keeps ten million serving-men,
   Who get no rest at all!
She sends 'em abroad on her own affairs,
   From the second she opens her eyes—
One million Hows, two million Wheres,
   And seven million Whys!

2

RIKKI-TIKKI-TAVI

'Rikki-Tikki-Tavi'
At the hole where he went in
Red-Eye called to Wrinkle-Skin.
Hear what little Red-Eye saith:
'Nag, come up and dance with death!'
Eye to eye and head to head,
(Keep the measure, Nag.)
This shall end when one is dead;
(At thy pleasure, Nag.)
Turn for turn and twist for twist—
(Run and hide thee, Nag.)
Hah! The hooded Death has missed!
(Woe betide thee, Nag!)

This is the story of the great war that Rikki-tikki-tavi fought single-handed, through the bath-rooms of the big bungalow in Segowlee cantonment. Darzee, the Tailorbird, helped him, and Chuchundra, the musk-rat, who never comes out into the middle of the floor, but always creeps round by the wall, gave him advice, but Rikki-tikki did the real fighting.

He was a mongoose, rather like a little cat in his fur and his tail, but quite like a weasel in his head and his habits. His eyes and the end of his restless nose were pink. He could scratch himself anywhere he pleased with any leg, front or back, that he chose to use. He could fluff up his tail till it looked like a bottle brush, and his war cry as he scuttled through the long grass was: 'Rikk-tikk-tikki-tikki-tchk!'

One day, a high summer flood washed him out of the burrow where he lived with his father and mother, and carried him, kicking and clucking, down a roadside ditch. He found a little wisp of grass floating there, and clung to it till he lost his senses. When he revived, he was lying in the hot sun on the middle of a garden path, very draggled indeed, and a small boy was saying, 'Here's a dead mongoose. Let's have a funeral.'

'No,' said his mother, 'let's take him in and dry him. Perhaps he isn't really dead.'

They took him into the house, and a big man picked him up between his finger and thumb and said he was not dead but half choked. So they wrapped him in cotton wool, and warmed him over a little fire, and he opened his eyes and sneezed.

'Now,' said the big man (he was an Englishman who had just moved into the bungalow), 'don't frighten him, and we'll see what he'll do.'

It is the hardest thing in the world to frighten a mongoose, because he is eaten up from nose to tail with curiosity. The motto of all the mongoose family is 'Run and find out', and Rikki-tikki was a true mongoose. He looked at the cotton wool, decided that it was not good to eat, ran all round the table, sat up and put his fur in order, scratched himself, and jumped on the small boy's shoulder.

'Don't be frightened, Teddy,' said his father. 'That's his way of making friends.'

'Ouch! He's tickling under my chin,' said Teddy.

Rikki-tikki looked down between the boy's collar and neck, snuffed at his ear, and climbed down to the floor, where he sat rubbing his nose.

'Good gracious,' said Teddy's mother, 'and that's a wild creature! I suppose he's so tame because we've been kind to him.'

'All mongooses are like that,' said her husband. 'If Teddy doesn't pick him up by the tail, or try to put him in a cage, he'll run in and out of the house all day long. Let's give him something to eat.'

They gave him a little piece of raw meat. Rikki-tikki liked it immensely, and when it was finished he went out into the veranda and sat in the sunshine and fluffed up his fur to make it dry to the roots. Then he felt better.

'There are more things to find out about in this house,' he said to himself, 'than all my family could find out in all their lives. I shall certainly stay and find out.'

He spent all that day roaming over the house. He nearly drowned himself in the bath-tubs, put his nose into the ink on a writing table, and burned it on the end of the big man's cigar, for he climbed up in the big man's lap to see how writing was done. At nightfall he ran into Teddy's nursery to watch how kerosene lamps were lighted, and when Teddy went to bed Rikki-tikki climbed up too. But he was a restless companion, because he had to get up and attend to every noise all through the night, and find out what made it.

Teddy's mother and father came in, the last thing, to look at their boy, and Rikki-tikki was awake on the pillow.

'I don't like that,' said Teddy's mother. 'He may bite the child.'

'He'll do no such thing,' said the father. 'Teddy's safer with that little beast than if he had a bloodhound to watch him. If a snake came into the nursery now—'

But Teddy's mother wouldn't think of anything so awful.

Early in the morning Rikki-tikki came to early breakfast in the veranda riding on Teddy's shoulder, and they gave him banana and some boiled egg. He sat on all their laps one after the other, because every well-brought-up mongoose always hopes to be a house mongoose some day and have rooms to run about in; and Rikki-tikki's mother (she used to live in the general's house at Segowlee) had carefully told Rikki what to do if ever he came across white men.

Then Rikki-tikki went out into the garden to see what was to be seen. It was a large garden, only half cultivated, with bushes, as big as summer-houses, of Marshal Niel roses, lime and orange trees, clumps of bamboos, and thickets of high grass.

Rikki-tikki licked his lips. 'This is a splendid hunting-ground,' he said, and his tail grew bottle-brushy at the thought of it, and he scuttled up and down the garden, snuffing here and there till he heard very sorrowful voices in a thorn-bush.

It was Darzee, the Tailorbird, and his wife. They had made a beautiful nest by pulling two big leaves together and stitching them up the edges with fibres, and had filled the hollow with cotton and downy fluff. The nest swayed to and fro, as they sat on the rim and cried.

'What is the matter?' asked Rikki-tikki.

'We are very miserable,' said Darzee. 'One of our babies fell out of the nest yesterday and Nag ate him.'

'H'm!' said Rikki-tikki, 'that is very sad—but I am a stranger here. Who is Nag?'

Darzee and his wife only cowered down in the nest without answering, for from the thick grass at the foot of the bush there came a low hiss—a horrid cold sound that made Rikki-tikki jump back two clear feet. Then inch by inch out of the grass rose up the head and spread hood of Nag, the big black cobra, and he was five feet long from tongue to tail. When he had lifted one-third of himself clear of the ground, he stayed balancing to and fro exactly as a dandelion tuft balances in the wind, and he looked at Rikki-tikki with the wicked snake's eyes that never change their expression, whatever the snake may be thinking of.

'Who is Nag?' said he. 'I am Nag. The great God Brahm put his mark upon all our people, when the first cobra spread his hood to keep the sun off Brahm as he slept. Look, and be afraid!'

He spread out his hood more than ever, and Rikki-tikki saw the spectacle-mark on the back of it that looks exactly like the eye part of a hook-and-eye fastening. He was afraid for the minute, but it is impossible for a mongoose to stay frightened for any length of time, and though Rikki-tikki had never met a live cobra before, his mother had fed him on dead ones, and he knew that all a grown mongoose's business in life was to fight and eat snakes. Nag knew that too and, at the bottom of his cold heart, he was afraid.

'Well,' said Rikki-tikki, and his tail began to fluff up again, 'marks or no marks, do you think it is right for you to eat fledglings out of a nest?'

Nag was thinking to himself, and watching the least little movement in the grass behind Rikki-tikki. He knew that mongooses in the garden meant death sooner or later for him and his family, but he wanted to get Rikki-tikki off his guard. So he dropped his head a little, and put it on one side.

'Let us talk,' he said.

'You eat eggs. Why should not I eat birds?'

'Behind you! Look behind you!' sang Darzee.

Rikki-tikki knew better than to waste time in staring. He jumped up in the air as high as he could go, and just under him whizzed by the head of Nagaina, Nag's wicked wife. She had crept up behind him as he was talking, to make an end of him. He heard her savage hiss as the stroke missed. He came down almost across her back, and if he had been an old mongoose he would have known that then was the time to break her back with one bite; but he was afraid of the terrible lashing return stroke of the cobra. He bit, indeed, but did not bite long enough, and he jumped clear of the whisking tail, leaving Nagaina torn and angry.

'Wicked, wicked Darzee!' said Nag, lashing up as high as he

could reach toward the nest in the thorn-bush. But Darzee had built it out of reach of snakes, and it only swayed to and fro.

Rikki-tikki felt his eyes growing red and hot (when a mongoose's eyes grow red, he is angry), and he sat back on his tail and hind-legs like a little kangaroo, and looked all round him, and chattered with rage. But Nag and Nagaina had disappeared into the grass. When a snake misses its stroke, it never says anything or gives any sign of what it means to do next. Rikki-tikki did not care to follow them, for he did not feel sure that he could manage two snakes at once. So he trotted off to the gravel path near the house, and sat down to think. It was a serious matter for him.

If you read the old books of natural history, you will find they say that when the mongoose fights the snake and happens to get bitten, he runs off and eats some herb that cures him. That is not true. The victory is only a matter of quickness of eye and quickness of foot—snake's blow against mongoose's jump—and as no eye can follow the motion of a snake's head when it strikes, this makes things much more wonderful than any magic herb. Rikki-tikki knew he was a young mongoose, and it made him all the more pleased to think that he had managed to escape a blow from behind. It gave him confidence in himself, and when Teddy came running down the path, Rikki-tikki was ready to be petted.

But just as Teddy was stooping, something wriggled a little in the dust, and a tiny voice said: 'Be careful. I am Death!' It was Karait, the dusty brown snakeling that lies for choice on the dusty earth; and his bite is as dangerous as the cobra's. But he is so small that nobody thinks of him, and so he does the more harm to people.

Rikki-tikki's eyes grew red again, and he danced up to Karait with the peculiar rocking, swaying motion that he had inherited from his family. It looks very funny, but it is so perfectly balanced a gait that you can fly off from it at any angle you please, and in dealing with snakes this is an advantage. If Rikki-tikki had only known, he was doing a much more dangerous thing than fighting Nag, for Karait is so small, and can turn so quickly, that unless Rikki bit him close to the back of the head, he would get the return stroke in his eye or his lip. But Rikki did not know. His eyes were all red, and he rocked back and forth, looking for a good place to hold. Karait struck out. Rikki jumped sideways and tried to run in, but the wicked little dusty grey head lashed within a fraction of his shoulder, and he had to jump over the body, and the head followed his heels close.

Teddy shouted to the house: 'Oh, look here! Our mongoose is killing a snake.' And Rikki-tikki heard a scream from Teddy's mother. His father ran out with a stick, but by the time he came up, Karait had lunged out once too far, and Rikki-tikki had sprung, jumped on the snake's back, dropped his head far between his forelegs, bitten as high up the back as he could get hold, and rolled away. That bite paralyzed Karait, and Rikki-tikki was just going to eat him up from the tail, after the custom of his family at dinner, when he remembered that a full meal makes a slow mongoose, and if he wanted all his strength and quickness ready, he must keep himself thin.

He went away for a dust bath under the castor-oil bushes, while Teddy's father beat the dead Karait. 'What is the use of that?' thought Rikki-tikki. 'I have settled it all;' and then Teddy's mother picked him up from the dust and hugged him, crying that he had saved Teddy from death, and Teddy's father said that he was a providence, and Teddy looked on with big scared eyes. Rikki-tikki was rather amused at all the fuss, which, of course, he did not understand. Teddy's mother might just as well have petted Teddy for playing in the dust. Rikki was thoroughly enjoying himself.

That night at dinner, walking to and fro among the wine-glasses on the table, he might have stuffed himself three times over with nice things. But he remembered Nag and Nagaina, and though it was very pleasant to be patted and petted by Teddy's mother, and to sit on Teddy's shoulder, his eyes would get red from time to time, and he would go off into his long war cry of 'Rikk-tikk-tikki-tikki-tchk!'

Teddy carried him off to bed, and insisted on Rikki-tikki sleeping under his chin. Rikki-tikki was too well bred to bite or scratch, but as soon as Teddy was asleep he went off for his nightly walk round the house, and in the dark he ran up against Chuchundra, the musk-rat, creeping around by the wall. Chuchundra is a broken-hearted little beast. He whimpers and cheeps all the night, trying to make up his mind to run into the middle of the room. But he never gets there.

'Don't kill me,' said Chuchundra, almost weeping. 'Rikki-tikki, don't kill me!'

'Do you think a snake-killer kills musk-rats?' said Rikki-tikki scornfully.

'Those who kill snakes get killed by snakes,' said Chuchundra, more sorrowfully than ever. 'And how am I to be sure that Nag won't mistake me for you some dark night?'

'There's not the least danger,' said Rikki-tikki. 'But Nag is in the garden, and I know you don't go there.'

'My cousin Chua, the rat, told me—' said Chuchundra, and then he stopped.

'Told you what?'

'H'sh! Nag is everywhere, Rikki-tikki. You should have talked to Chua in the garden.'

'I didn't—so you must tell me. Quick, Chuchundra, or I'll bite you!'

Chuchundra sat down and cried till the tears rolled off his whiskers. 'I am a very poor man,' he sobbed. 'I never had spirit enough to run out into the middle of the room. H'sh! I mustn't tell you anything. Can't you hear, Rikki-tikki?'

Rikki-tikki listened. The house was as still as still, but he thought he could just catch the faintest scratch-scratch in the world—a noise as faint as that of a wasp walking on a window-pane—the dry scratch of a snake's scales on brick-work.

'That's Nag or Nagaina,' he said to himself, 'and he is crawling into the bath-room sluice. You're right, Chuchundra; I should have talked to Chua.'

He stole off to Teddy's bathroom, but there was nothing there, and then to Teddy's mother's bathroom. At the bottom of the smooth plaster wall there was a brick pulled out to make a sluice for the bath water, and as Rikki-tikki stole in by the masonry curb where the bath is put, he heard Nag and Nagaina whispering together outside in the moonlight.

'When the house is emptied of people,' said Nagaina to her husband, 'he will have to go away, and then the garden will be our own again. Go in quietly, and remember that the big man who killed Karait is the first one to bite. Then come out and tell me, and we will hunt for Rikki-tikki together.'

'But are you sure that there is anything to be gained by killing the people?' said Nag.

'Everything. When there were no people in the bungalow, did we have any mongoose in the garden? So long as the bungalow is empty, we are king and queen of the garden; and remember that as soon as our eggs in the melon bed hatch (as they may tomorrow), our children will need room and quiet.'

'I had not thought of that,' said Nag. 'I will go, but there is no need that we should hunt for Rikki-tikki afterward. I will kill the big man and his wife, and the child if I can, and come away quietly. Then the bungalow will be empty, and Rikki-tikki will go.'

Rikki-tikki tingled all over with rage and hatred at this, and then Nag's head came through the sluice, and his five feet of cold body followed it. Angry as he was, Rikki-tikki was very frightened as he saw the size of the big cobra. Nag coiled himself up, raised his head, and looked into the bathroom in the dark, and Rikki could see his eyes glitter.

'Now, if I kill him here, Nagaina will know; and if I fight him on the open floor, the odds are in his favour. What am I to do?' said Rikki-tikki-tavi.

Nag waved to and fro, and then Rikki-tikki heard him drinking from the biggest water jar that was used to fill the bath. 'That is good,' said the snake. 'Now, when Karait was killed, the big man had a stick. He may have that stick still, but when he comes in to bathe in the morning he will not have a stick. I shall wait here till he comes. Nagaina—do you hear me?—I shall wait here in the cool till daytime.'

There was no answer from outside, so Rikki-tikki knew Nagaina had gone away. Nag coiled himself down, coil by coil, round the bulge at the bottom of the water jar, and Rikki-tikki stayed still as death. After an hour he began to move, muscle by muscle, toward the jar. Nag was asleep, and Rikki-tikki looked at his big back, wondering which would be the best place for a good hold.

'If I don't break his back at the first jump,' said Rikki, 'he can still fight. And if he fights—O Rikki!' He looked at the thickness of the neck below the hood, but that was too much for him; and a bite near the tail would only make Nag savage. 'It must be the head,' he said at last; 'the head above the hood. And, when I am once there, I must not let go.'

Then he jumped. The head was lying a little clear of the water jar, under the curve of it; and, as his teeth met, Rikki braced his back against the bulge of the red earthenware to hold down the head. This gave him just one second's purchase, and he made the most of it. Then he was battered to and fro as a rat is shaken by a dog—to and fro on the floor, up and down, and around in great circles, but his eyes were red and he held on as the body cart-whipped over the floor, upsetting the tin dipper and the soap dish and the flesh brush, and banged against the tin side of the bath. As he held he closed his jaws tighter and tighter, for he made sure he would be banged to death, and, for the honour of his family, he preferred to be found with his teeth locked. He was dizzy, aching, and felt shaken to pieces when something went off like a thunderclap just behind him. A hot wind knocked him senseless and red fire singed his fur.

The big man had been wakened by the noise, and had fired both barrels of a shotgun into Nag just behind the hood. Rikki-tikki held on with his eyes shut, for now he was quite sure he was dead. But the head did not move, and the big man picked him up and said, 'It's the mongoose again, Alice. The little chap has saved our lives now.'

Then Teddy's mother came in with a very white face, and saw what was left of Nag, and Rikki-tikki dragged himself to Teddy's bedroom and spent half the rest of the night shaking himself tenderly to find out whether he really was broken into forty pieces, as he fancied.

When morning came he was very stiff, but well pleased with his doings. 'Now I have Nagaina to settle with, and she will be worse than five Nags, and there's no knowing when the eggs she spoke of will hatch. Goodness! I must go and see Darzee,' he said.

Without waiting for breakfast, Rikki-tikki ran to the thorn-bush where Darzee was singing a song of triumph at the top of his voice. The news of Nag's death was all over the garden, for the sweeper had thrown the body on the rubbish heap.

'Oh, you stupid tuft of feathers!' said Rikki-tikki angrily. 'Is this the time to sing?'

'Nag is dead—is dead—is dead!' sang Darzee. 'The valiant Rikki-tikki caught him by the head and held fast. The big man brought the bang-stick, and Nag fell in two pieces! He will never eat my babies again.'

'All that's true enough. But where's Nagaina?' said Rikki-tikki, looking carefully round him.

'Nagaina came to the bathroom sluice and called for Nag,'

Darzee went on, 'and Nag came out on the end of a stick—the sweeper picked him up on the end of a stick and threw him upon the rubbish heap. Let us sing about the great, the red-eyed Rikki-tikki!' And Darzee filled his throat and sang.

'If I could get up to your nest, I'd roll your babies out!' said Rikki-tikki. 'You don't know when to do the right thing at the right time. You're safe enough in your nest there, but it's war for me down here. Stop singing a minute, Darzee.'

'For the great, the beautiful Rikki-tikki's sake I will stop,' said Darzee. 'What is it, O Killer of the terrible Nag?'

'Where is Nagaina, for the third time?' 'On the rubbish heap by the stables, mourning for Nag. Great is Rikki-tikki with the white teeth.'

'Bother my white teeth! Have you ever heard where she keeps her eggs?'

'In the melon bed, on the end nearest the wall, where the sun strikes nearly all day. She hid them there weeks ago.'

'And you never thought it worth while to tell me? The end nearest the wall, you said?'

'Rikki-tikki, you are not going to eat her eggs?'

'Not eat exactly; no. Darzee, if you have a grain of sense you will fly off to the stables and pretend that your wing is broken, and let Nagaina chase you away to this bush. I must get to the melon bed, and if I went there now she'd see me.'

Darzee was a feather-brained little fellow who could never hold more than one idea at a time in his head. And just because he knew that Nagaina's children were born in eggs like his own, he didn't think at first that it was fair to kill them. But his wife was a sensible bird, and she knew that cobra's eggs meant young cobras later on. So she flew off from the nest, and left Darzee to keep the babies warm, and continue his song about the death of Nag. Darzee was very like a man in some ways.

She fluttered in front of Nagaina by the rubbish heap and

cried out, 'Oh, my wing is broken! The boy in the house threw a stone at me and broke it.' Then she fluttered more desperately than ever.

Nagaina lifted up her head and hissed, 'You warned Rikki-tikki when I would have killed him. Indeed and truly, you've chosen a bad place to be lame in.' And she moved toward Darzee's wife, slipping along over the dust.

'The boy broke it with a stone!' shrieked Darzee's wife.

'Well! It may be some consolation to you when you're dead to know that I shall settle accounts with the boy. My husband lies on the rubbish heap this morning, but before night the boy in the house will lie very still. What is the use of running away? I am sure to catch you. Little fool, look at me!'

Darzee's wife knew better than to do that, for a bird who looks at a snake's eyes gets so frightened that she cannot move. Darzee's wife fluttered on, piping sorrowfully, and never leaving the ground, and Nagaina quickened her pace.

Rikki-tikki heard them going up the path from the stables, and he raced for the end of the melon patch near the wall.

There, in the warm litter above the melons, very cunningly hidden, he found twenty-five eggs, about the size of a bantam's eggs, but with whitish skin instead of shell.

'I was not a day too soon,' he said, for he could see the baby cobras curled up inside the skin, and he knew that the minute they were hatched they could each kill a man or a mongoose. He bit off the tops of the eggs as fast as he could, taking care to crush the young cobras, and turned over the litter from time to time to see whether he had missed any. At last there were only three eggs left, and Rikki-tikki began to chuckle to himself, when he heard Darzee's wife screaming: 'Rikki-tikki, I led Nagaina toward the house, and she has gone into the veranda, and—oh, come quickly—she means killing!' Rikki-tikki smashed two eggs, and tumbled backward down the melon bed with the third egg in his mouth, and scuttled to the veranda as hard as he could put foot to the ground.

Teddy and his mother and father were there at early breakfast, but Rikki-tikki saw that they were not eating anything. They sat stone-still, and their faces were white. Nagaina was coiled up on the matting by Teddy's chair, within easy striking distance of Teddy's bare leg, and she was swaying to and fro, singing a song of triumph.

'Son of the big man that killed Nag,' she hissed, 'stay still. I am not ready yet. Wait a little. Keep very still, all you three! If you move I strike, and if you do not move I strike. Oh, foolish people, who killed my Nag!'

Teddy's eyes were fixed on his father, and all his father could do was to whisper, 'Sit still, Teddy. You mustn't move. Teddy, keep still.'

Then Rikki-tikki came up and cried, 'Turn round, Nagaina. Turn and fight!'

'All in good time,' said she, without moving her eyes. 'I will settle my account with you presently. Look at your friends, Rikki-tikki. They are still and white. They are afraid. They dare not move, and if you come a step nearer I strike.'

'Look at your eggs,' said Rikki-tikki, 'in the melon bed near the wall. Go and look, Nagaina!'

The big snake turned half around, and saw the egg on the veranda. 'Ah-h! Give it to me,' she said.

Rikki-tikki put his paws one on each side of the egg, and his eyes were blood-red. 'What price for a snake's egg? For a young cobra? For a young king cobra? For the last—the very last of the brood? The ants are eating all the others down by the melon bed.'

Nagaina spun clear round, forgetting everything for the sake of the one egg. Rikki-tikki saw Teddy's father shoot out a big hand, catch Teddy by the shoulder, and drag him across the little table with the tea-cups, safe and out of reach of Nagaina.

'Tricked! Tricked! Tricked! Rikk-tck-tck!' chuckled Rikki-tikki. 'The boy is safe, and it was I—I—I that caught Nag by the hood last night in the bathroom.' Then he began to jump up and down, all four feet together, his head close to the floor. 'He threw me to and fro, but he could not shake me off. He was dead before the big man blew him in two. I did it! Rikki-tikki-tck-tck! Come then, Nagaina. Come and fight with me. You shall not be a widow long.'

Nagaina saw that she had lost her chance of killing Teddy, and the egg lay between Rikki-tikki's paws. 'Give me the egg, Rikki-tikki. Give me the last of my eggs, and I will go away and never come back,' she said, lowering her hood.

'Yes, you will go away, and you will never come back. For you will go to the rubbish heap with Nag. Fight, widow! The big man has gone for his gun! Fight!'

Rikki-tikki was bounding all round Nagaina, keeping just out of reach of her stroke, his little eyes like hot coals. Nagaina gathered herself together and flung out at him. Rikki-tikki jumped up and backward. Again and again and again she struck, and each time her head came with a whack on the matting of the veranda and she gathered herself together like a watch spring. Then Rikki-tikki danced in a circle to get behind her, and Nagaina spun round to keep her head to his head, so that the rustle of her tail on the matting sounded like dry leaves blown along by the wind. He had forgotten the egg. It still lay on the veranda, and Nagaina came nearer and nearer to it, till at last, while Rikki-tikki was drawing breath, she caught it in her mouth, turned to the veranda steps, and flew like an arrow down the path, with Rikki-tikki behind her. When the cobra runs for her life, she goes like a whip-lash flicked across a horse's neck. Rikki-tikki knew that he must catch her, or all the trouble would begin again. She headed straight for the long grass by the thorn-bush, and as he was running Rikki-tikki heard Darzee still singing his foolish little song of triumph.

But Darzee's wife was wiser. She flew off her nest as Nagaina came along, and flapped her wings about Nagaina's head. If Darzee had helped they might have turned her, but Nagaina only lowered her hood and went on. Still, the instant's delay brought Rikki-tikki up to her, and as she plunged into the rat-hole where she and Nag used to live, his little white teeth were clenched on her tail, and he went down with her—and very few mongooses, however wise and old they may be, care to follow a cobra into its hole. It was dark in the hole; and Rikki-tikki never knew when it might open out and give Nagaina room to turn and strike at him. He held on savagely, and stuck out his feet to act as brakes on the dark slope of the hot, moist earth.

Then the grass by the mouth of the hole stopped waving, and Darzee said, 'It is all over with Rikki-tikki! We must sing his death song. Valiant Rikki-tikki is dead! For Nagaina will surely kill him underground.' So he sang a very mournful song that he made up on the spur of the minute, and just as he got to the most touching part, the grass quivered again, and Rikki-tikki, covered with dirt, dragged himself out of the hole leg by leg, licking his whiskers.

Darzee stopped with a little shout. Rikki-tikki shook some of the dust out of his fur and sneezed. 'It is all over,' he said. 'The widow will never come out again.' And the red ants that live between the grass stems heard him, and began to troop down one after another to see if he had spoken the truth.

Rikki-tikki curled himself up in the grass and slept where he was—slept and slept till it was late in the afternoon, for he had done a hard day's work. 'Now,' he said, when he awoke, 'I will go back to the house. Tell the Coppersmith, Darzee, and he will tell the garden that Nagaina is dead.'

The Coppersmith is a bird who makes a noise exactly like the beating of a little hammer on a copper pot; and the reason he is always making it is because he is the town crier to every Indian garden, and tells all the news to everybody who cares to listen. As Rikki-tikki went up the path, he heard his 'attention' notes like a tiny dinner gong, and then the steady 'Ding-dong-tock! Nag is dead—dong! Nagaina is dead! Ding-dong-tock!' That set all the birds in the garden singing, and the frogs croaking, for Nag and Nagaina used to eat frogs as well as little birds.

When Rikki got to the house, Teddy and Teddy's mother (she looked very white still, for she had been fainting) and Teddy's father came out and almost cried over him; and that night he ate all that was given him till he could eat no more, and went to bed on Teddy's shoulder, where Teddy's mother saw him when she came to look late at night. 'He saved our lives and Teddy's life,' she said to her husband. 'Just think, he saved all our lives.'

Rikki-tikki woke up with a jump, for the mongooses are light sleepers. 'Oh, it's you,' said he. 'What are you bothering for? All the cobras are dead. And if they weren't, I'm here.'

Rikki-tikki had a right to be proud of himself. But he did not grow too proud, and he kept that garden as a mongoose should keep it, with tooth and jump and spring and bite, till never a cobra dared show its head inside the walls.

3

HOW THE LEOPARD GOT HIS SPOTS

In the days when everybody started fair, Best Beloved, the Leopard lived in a place called the High Veldt.[1] 'Member it wasn't the Low Veldt, or the Bush Veldt, or the Sour Veldt, but the 'sclusively bare, hot, shiny High Veldt, where there was sand and sandy-coloured rock and 'sclusively tufts of sandy-yellowish grass. The Giraffe and the Zebra and the Eland and the Koodoo and the Hartebeest lived there; and they were 'sclusively sandy-yellow-brownish all over; but the Leopard, he was the 'sclusivest sandiest-yellowest-brownest of them all—a greyish-yellowish catty-shaped kind of beast, and he matched the 'sclusively yellowish-greyish-brownish colour of the High Veldt to one hair. This was very bad for the Giraffe and the Zebra and the rest of them; for he would lie down by a 'sclusively yellowish-greyish-brownish stone or clump of grass, and when the Giraffe or the Zebra or the Eland or the Koodoo or the Bush-Buck or the Bonte-Buck[2] came by he would surprise them out of their jumpsome lives. He would indeed! And, also, there was an Ethiopian with bows and arrows (a 'sclusively greyish-brownish-yellowish man he was then), who lived on the High Veldt with the Leopard; and the two used to hunt together—the Ethiopian with his bows and arrows, and the Leopard 'sclusively with his teeth and claws—till the Giraffe and the Eland and the Koodoo and the Quagga[3] and all the rest of them didn't know which way to jump,

Best Beloved. They didn't indeed!

After a long time—things lived for ever so long in those days—they learned to avoid anything that looked like a Leopard or an Ethiopian; and bit by bit—the Giraffe began it, because his legs were the longest—they went away from the High Veldt. They scuttled for days and days and days till they came to a great forest, 'sclusively full of trees and bushes and stripy, speckly, patchy-blatchy shadows, and there they hid, and after another long time, what with standing half in the shade and half out of it, and what with the slippery-slidy shadows of the trees falling on them, the Giraffe grew blotchy, and the Zebra grew stripy, and the Eland and the Koodoo grew darker, with little wavy grey lines on their backs like bark on a tree trunk; and so, though you could hear them and smell them, you could very seldom see them, and then only when you knew precisely where to look. They had a beautiful time in the 'sclusively speckly-spickly shadows of the forest, while the Leopard and the Ethiopian ran about over the 'sclusively greyish-yellowish-reddish High Veldt outside, wondering where all their breakfasts and their dinners and their teas had gone. At last they were so hungry that they ate rats and beetles and rock-rabbits, the Leopard and the Ethiopian, and then they had the Big Tummy-ache, both together; and then they met Baviaan—the dog-headed, barking Baboon, who is Quite the Wisest Animal in All South Africa.

Said Leopard to Baviaan (and it was a very hot day), 'Where has all the game gone?'

And Baviaan winked. *He* knew.

Said the Ethiopian to Baviaan, 'Can you tell me the present habitat of the aboriginal Fauna?' (That meant just the same thing, but the Ethiopian always used long words. He was a grown-up.)

And Baviaan winked. *He* knew.

Then said Baviaan, 'The game has gone into other spots; and my advice to you, Leopard, is to go into other spots as soon as you can.'

And the Ethiopian said, 'That is all very fine, but I wish to know whither the aboriginal Fauna has migrated.'

Then said Baviaan, 'The aboriginal Fauna has joined the aboriginal Flora because it was high time for a change; and my advice to you, Ethiopian, is to change as soon as you can.'

That puzzled the Leopard and the Ethiopian, but they set off to look for the aboriginal Flora, and presently, after ever so many days, they saw a great, high, tall forest full of tree trunks all 'sclusively speckled and sprottled and spotted, dotted and splashed and slashed and hatched and cross-hatched with shadows. (Say that quickly aloud, and you will see how *very* shadowy the forest must have been.)

'What is this,' said the Leopard, 'that is so 'sclusively dark, and yet so full of little pieces of light?'

'I don't know,' said the Ethiopian, 'but it ought to be the aboriginal Flora. I can smell Giraffe, and I can hear Giraffe, but I can't see Giraffe.'

'That's curious,' said the Leopard. 'I suppose it is because we have just come in out of the sunshine. I can smell Zebra, and I can hear Zebra, but I can't see Zebra.'

'Wait a bit,' said the Ethiopian. 'It's a long time since we've hunted 'em. Perhaps we've forgotten what they were like.'

'Fiddle!' said the Leopard. 'I remember them perfectly on the High Veldt, especially their marrow-bones. Giraffe is about seventeen feet high, of a 'sclusively fulvous[4] golden-yellow from head to heel; and Zebra is about four and a half feet high, of a 'sclusively grey-fawn colour from head to heel.'

'Umm,' said the Ethiopian, looking into the speckly-spickly shadows of the aboriginal Flora, forest. 'Then they ought to show up in this dark place like ripe bananas in a smokehouse.'

But they didn't. The Leopard and the Ethiopian hunted all day; and though they could smell them and hear them, they never saw one of them.

'For goodness' sake,' said the Leopard at teatime, 'let us wait till it gets dark. This daylight hunting is a perfect scandal.'

So they waited till dark, and then the Leopard heard something breathing sniffily in the starlight that fell all stripy through the branches, and he jumped at the noise, and it smelt like Zebra, and it felt like Zebra, and when he knocked it down it kicked like Zebra, but he couldn't see it. So he said, 'Be quiet, O you person without any form. I am going to sit on your head till morning, because there is something about you that I don't understand.'

Presently he heard a grunt and a crash and a scramble, and the Ethiopian called out, 'I've caught a thing that I can't see. It smells like Giraffe, and it kicks like Giraffe, but it hasn't any form.'

'Don't you trust it,' said the Leopard. 'Sit on its head till the morning—same as me. They haven't any form—any of 'em.'

So they sat down on them hard till bright morning time, and then Leopard said, 'What have you at your end of the table, Brother?'

The Ethiopian scratched his head and said, 'It ought to be 'sclusively a rich fulvous orange-tawny from head to heel, and it ought to be Giraffe; but it is covered all over with chestnut blotches. What have you at *your* end of the table, Brother?'

And the Leopard scratched his head and said, 'It ought to be 'sclusively a delicate greyish-fawn, and it ought to be Zebra; but it is covered all over with black and purple stripes. What in the world have you been doing to yourself Zebra? Don't you know that if you were in the High Veldt I could see you ten miles off? You haven't any form.'

'Yes,' said the Zebra, 'but this isn't the High Veldt. Can't you see?'

'I can now,' said the Leopard. 'But I couldn't all yesterday. How is it done?'

'Let us up,' said the Zebra, 'and we will show you.'

They let the Zebra and the Giraffe get up; and Zebra moved

away to some little thorn bushes where the sunlight fell all stripy, and Giraffe moved off to some tallish trees where the shadows fell all blotchy.

'Now watch,' said the Zebra and the Giraffe. 'This is the way it's done. One—two—three! And where's your breakfast?'

Leopard stared, and Ethiopian stared, but all they could see were stripy shadows and blotched shadows in the forest, but never a sign of Zebra and Giraffe. They had just walked off and hidden themselves in the shadowy forest.

'Hi! Hi!' said the Ethiopian. 'That's a trick worth learning. Take a lesson by it, Leopard. You show up in this dark place like a bar of soap in a coal scuttle.'

'Ho! Ho!' said the Leopard. 'Would it surprise you very much to know that you show up in this dark place like a mustard plaster on a sack of coals?'

'Well, calling names won't catch dinner,' said the Ethiopian. 'The long and the little of it is that we don't match our backgrounds. I'm going to take Baviaan's advice. He told me I ought to change; and as I've nothing to change except my skin I'm going to change that.'

'What to?' said the Leopard, tremendously excited.

'To a nice working blackish-brownish colour, with a little purple in it, and touches of slaty-blue. It will be the very thing for hiding in hollows and behind trees.'

So he changed his skin then and there, and the Leopard was more excited than ever; he had never seen a man change his skin before.

'But what about me?' he said, when the Ethiopian had worked his last little finger into his fine new black skin.

'You take Baviaan's advice too. He told you to go into spots.'

'So I did,' said the Leopard. 'I went into other spots as fast as I could. I went into this spot with you, and a lot of good it has done me.'

'Oh,' said the Ethiopian, 'Baviaan didn't mean spots in South Africa. He meant spots on your skin.'

'What's the use of that?' said the Leopard.

'Think of Giraffe,' said the Ethiopian. 'Or if you prefer stripes, think of Zebra. They find their spots and stripes give them per-fect satisfaction.'

'Umm,' said the Leopard. 'I wouldn't look like Zebra—not for ever so.'

'Well, make up your mind,' said the Ethiopian, 'because I'd hate to go hunting without you, but I must if you insist on looking like a sunflower against a tarred fence.'

'I'll take spots, then,' said the Leopard; 'but don't make 'em too vulgar-big. I wouldn't look like Giraffe—not for ever so.'

'I'll make 'em with the tips of my fingers,' said the Ethiopian. 'There's plenty of black left on my skin still. Stand over!'

Then the Ethiopian put his five fingers close together (there was plenty of black left on his new skin still) and pressed them all over the Leopard, and wherever the five fingers touched they left five little black marks, all close together. You can see them on any Leopard's skin you like, Best Beloved. Sometimes the fingers slipped and the marks got a little blurred; but if you look closely at any Leopard now you will see that there are always five spots—off five fat black fingertips.

'Now you *are* a beauty!' said the Ethiopian. 'You can lie out on the bare ground and look like a heap of pebbles. You can lie out on the naked rocks and look like a piece of puddingstone.⁵ You can lie out on a leafy branch and look like sunshine sifting through the leaves; and you can lie right across the centre of a path and look like nothing in particular. Think of that and purr!'

'But if I'm all this,' said the Leopard, 'why didn't you go spotty too?'

'Oh, plain black's best for a nigger,' said the Ethiopian. 'Now come along and we'll see if we can't get even with

Mr One-Two-Three-Where's-your-Breakfast!'

So they went away and lived happily ever afterward, Best Beloved. That is all.

Oh, now and then you will hear grown-ups say, 'Can the Ethiopian change his skin or the Leopard his spots?'[6] I don't think even grown-ups would keep on saying such a silly thing if the Leopard and the Ethiopian hadn't done it once—do you? But they will never do it again, Best Beloved. They are quite contented as they are.

> *I am the Most Wise Baviaan, saying in most wise tones,*
> *'Let us melt into the landscape—just us two by our lones.'*
> *People have come—in a carriage—calling. But Mummy is there...*
> *Yes, I can go if you take me—Nurse says she don't care.*
> *Let's go up to the pigsties and sit on the farmyard rails!*
> *Let's say things to the bunnies, and watch 'em skitter their tails!*
> *Let's—oh, anything, Daddy, so long as it's you and me,*
> *And going truly exploring, and not being in till tea!*
> *Here's your boots (I've brought 'em), and here's your cap and stick,*
> *And here's your pipe and tobacco. Oh, come along out of it—quick!*

4

BREAD UPON THE WATERS

If you remember my improper friend Brugglesmith, you will also bear in mind his friend McPhee, Chief Engineer of the *Breslau*, whose dingehy Brugglesmith tried to steal. His apologies for the performances of Brugglesmith may one day be told in their proper place: the tale before us concerns McPhee. He was never a racing engineer, and took special pride in saying as much before the Liverpool men; but he had a thirty-two years' knowledge of machinery and the humours of ships. One side of his face had been wrecked through the bursting of a pressure-gauge in the days when men knew less than they do now, and his nose rose grandly out of the wreck, like a club in a public riot. There were cuts and lumps on his head, and he would guide your forefinger through his short iron-grey hair and tell you how he had come by his trade-marks. He owned all sorts of certificates of extra-competency, and at the bottom of his cabin chest of drawers, where he kept the photograph of his wife, were two or three Royal Humane Society medals for saving lives at sea. Professionally—it was different when crazy steerage-passengers jumped overboard—professionally, McPhee does not approve of saving life at sea, and he has often told me that a new Hell awaits stokers and trimmers who sign for a strong man's pay and fall sick the second day out. He believes in throwing boots at fourth and fifth engineers when they wake him up at night with word that a bearing is red-hot, all because a lamp's glare is reflected red from the twirling metal. He believes that there are only two poets in the world: one being Robert Burns, of course, and the other Gerald Massey. When he has time for novels he reads Wilkie Collins and Charles Reade—chiefly the latter—and knows whole pages of *Hard Cash* by heart. In the saloon his table is next to the captain's, and he drinks only water while his engines work.

He was good to me when we first met, because I did not ask questions, and believed in Charles Reade as a most shamefully neglected author. Later he approved of my writings to the extent of one pamphlet of twenty-four pages that I wrote for Holdock, Steiner & Chase, owners of the line, when they bought some ventilating patent and fitted it to the cabins of the *Breslau*, *Spandau*, and *Koltzau*. The purser of the *Breslau* recommended me to Holdock's secretary for the job; and Holdock, who is a Wesleyan Methodist, invited me to his house, and gave me dinner with the governess when the others had finished, and placed the plans and specifications in my hand, and I wrote the pamphlet that same afternoon. It was called 'Comfort in the Cabin', and brought me seven pound ten, cash down—an important sum of money in those days; and the governess, who was teaching Master John Holdock his scales, told me that Mrs Holdock had told her to keep an eye on me, in case I went away with coats from the hat-rack. McPhee liked that pamphlet enormously, for it was composed in the Bouverie-Byzantine style, with baroque and rococo embellishments; and afterwards he introduced me to Mrs McPhee, who succeeded Dinah in my heart; for Dinah was half a world away, and it is wholesome and antiseptic to love such a woman as Janet McPhee. They lived in a little twelve-pound house, close to the shipping. When McPhee was away Mrs McPhee read the Lloyds column in the papers, and called on the wives of senior engineers of equal social standing. Once or twice, too, Mrs Holdock visited Mrs

McPhee in a brougham with celluloid fittings, and I have reason to believe that, after she had played owner's wife long enough, they talked scandal. The Holdocks lived in an old-fashioned house with a big brick garden not a mile from the McPhees, for they stayed by their money as their money stayed by them; and in summer you met their brougham solemnly junketing by Theydon Bois or Loughton. But I was Mrs McPhee's friend, for she allowed me to convoy her westward, sometimes, to theatres where she sobbed or laughed or shivered with a simple heart; and she introduced me to a new world of doctors' wives, captains' wives, and engineers' wives, whose whole talk and thought centred in and about ships and lines of ships you have never heard of. There were sailing-ships, with stewards and mahogany and maple saloons, trading to Australia, taking cargoes of consumptives and hopeless drunkards for whom a sea-voyage was recommended; there were frowzy little West African boats, full of rats and cockroaches, where men died anywhere but in their bunks; there were Brazilian boats whose cabins could be hired for merchandise, that went out loaded nearly awash; there were Zanzibar and Mauritius steamers and wonderful reconstructed boats that plied to the other tide of Borneo. These were loved and known, for they earned our bread and a little butter, and we despised the big Atlantic boats, and made fun of the P. & O. and Orient liners, and swore by our respective owners—Wesleyan, Baptist, or Presbyterian, as the case might be.

I had only just come back to England when Mrs McPhee invited me to dinner at three o'clock in the afternoon, and the notepaper was almost bridal in its scented creaminess. When I reached the house I saw that there were new curtains in the window that must have cost forty-five shillings a pair; and as Mrs McPhee drew me into the little marble-papered hall, she looked at me keenly, and cried:

'Have ye not heard? What d'ye think o' the hat-rack?'

Now, that hat-rack was oak—thirty shillings, at least. McPhee came down-stairs with a sober foot—he steps as lightly as a cat, for all his weight, when he is at sea—and shook hands in a new and awful manner—a parody of old Holdock's style when he says good-bye to his skippers. I perceived at once that a legacy had come to him, but I held my peace, though Mrs McPhee begged me every thirty seconds to eat a great deal and say nothing. It was rather a mad sort of meal, because McPhee and his wife took hold of hands like little children (they always do after voyages), and nodded and winked and choked and gurgled, and hardly ate a mouthful.

A female servant came in and waited; though Mrs McPhee had told me time and again that she would thank no one to do her housework while she had her health. But this was a servant with a cap, and I saw Mrs McPhee swell and swell under her garance-coloured gown. There is no small free-board to Janet McPhee, nor is garance any subdued tint; and with all this unexplained pride and glory in the air I felt like watching fireworks without knowing the festival. When the maid had removed the cloth she brought a pineapple that would have cost half a guinea at that season (only McPhee has his own way of getting such things), and a Canton china bowl of dried lichis, and a glass plate of preserved ginger, and a small jar of sacred and Imperial chow-chow that perfumed the room. McPhee gets it from a Dutchman in Java, and I think he doctors it with liqueurs. But the crown of the feast was some Madeira of the kind you can only come by if you know the wine and the man. A little maize-wrapped fig of clotted Madeira cigars went with the wine, and the rest was a pale-blue smoky silence; Janet, in her splendour, smiling on us two, and patting McPhee's hand.

'We'll drink,' said McPhee, slowly, rubbing his chin, 'to the eternal damnation o' Holdock, Steiner & Chase.'

Of course I answered 'Amen', though I had made seven pound ten shillings out of the firm. McPhee's enemies were mine, and I was drinking his Madeira.

'Ye've heard nothing?' said Janet. 'Not a word, not a whisper?'

'Not a word, nor a whisper. On my word, I have not.'

'Tell him, Mac,' said she; and that is another proof of Janet's goodness and wifely love. A smaller woman would have babbled first, but Janet is five feet nine in her stockings.

'We're rich,' said McPhee. I shook hands all round.

'We're damned rich,' he added. I shook hands all round a second time.

'I'll go to sea no more—unless—there's no sayin'—a private yacht, maybe—wi' a small an' handy auxiliary.'

'It's not enough for that,' said Janet. 'We're fair rich—well-to-do, but no more. A new gown for church, and one for the theatre. We'll have it made west.'

'How much is it? I asked.

'Twenty-five thousand pounds.' I drew a long breath. 'An' I've been earnin' twenty-five an' twenty pound a month!' The last words came away with a roar, as though the wide world was conspiring to beat him down.

'All this time I'm waiting,' I said. 'I know nothing since last September. Was it left you?'

They laughed aloud together. 'It was left,' said McPhee, choking. 'Ou, ay, it was left. That's vara good. Of course it was left. Janet, d'ye note that? It was left. Now if you'd put that in your pamphlet it would have been vara jocose. It was left.' He slapped his thigh and roared till the wine quivered in the decanter.

The Scotch are a great people, but they are apt to hang over a joke too long, particularly when no one can see the point but themselves.

'When I rewrite my pamphlet I'll put it in, McPhee. Only I must know something more first.'

McPhee thought for the length of half a cigar, while Janet caught my eye and led it round the room to one new thing after another—the new vine-pattern carpet, the new chiming rustic clock between the models of the Colombo outrigger-boats, the new inlaid sideboard with a purple cut-glass flower-stand, the fender of gilt and brass, and last, the new black-and-gold piano.

'In October o' last year the Board sacked me,' began McPhee. 'In October o' last year the *Breslau* came in for winter overhaul. She'd been runnin' eight months—two hunder an' forty days—an' I was three days makin' up my indents, when she went to dry-dock. All told, mark you, it was this side o' three hunder pound—to be preceese, two hunder an' eighty-six pound four shillings. There's not another man could ha' nursed the *Breslau* for eight months to that tune. Never again—never again! They may send their boats to the bottom, for aught I care.'

'There's no need,' said Janet, softly. 'We're done wi' Holdock, Steiner & Chase.'

'It's irritatin', Janet, it's just irritatin'. I ha' been justified from first to last, as the world knows, but—but I canna forgie 'em. Ay, wisdom is justified o' her children; an' any other man than me wad ha' made the indent eight hunder. Hay was our skipper— ye'll have met him. They shifted him to the *Torgau*, an' bade me wait for the *Breslau* under young Bannister. Ye'll obsairve there'd been a new election on the Board. I heard the shares were sellin' hither an' yon, an' the major part of the Board was new to me. The old Board would ne'er ha' done it. They trusted me. But the new Board were all for reorganization. Young Steiner—Steiner's son—the Jew, was at the bottom of it, an' they did not think it worth their while to send me word. The first I knew—an' I was Chief Engineer—was the notice of the line's winter sailin's, and the *Breslau* timed for sixteen days between port an' port! Sixteen days, man! She's a good boat, but eighteen is her summer time, mark you. Sixteen was sheer flytin', kitin' nonsense, an' so I told young Bannister.

'"We've got to make it," he said. "Ye should not ha' sent in a three hunder pound indent."

'Do they look for their boats to be run on air?' I said. 'The Board's daft.

"E'en tell 'em so," he says. "I'm a married man, an' my fourth's on the ways now, she says."'

'A boy—wi' red hair,' Janet put in. Her own hair is the splendid red-gold that goes with a creamy complexion.

'My word, I was an angry man that day! Forbye I was fond o' the old *Breslau*, I looked for a little consideration from the Board after twenty years' service. There was Board-meetin' on Wednesday, an' I slept overnight in the engine-room, takin' figures to support my case. Well, I put it fair and square before them all. "Gentlemen," I said, "I've run the *Breslau* eight seasons, an' I believe there's no fault to find wi' my wark. But if ye haud to this"—I waggled the advertisement at 'em—"this that I've never heard of it till I read it at breakfast, I do assure you on my professional reputation, she can never do it. That is to say, she can for a while, but at a risk no thinkin' man would run."

'"What the deil d'ye suppose we pass your indents for?" says old Holdock. "Man, we're spendin' money like watter."

'"I'll leave it in the Board's hands," I said, "if two hunder an' eighty-seven pound is anything beyond right and reason for eight months." I might ha' saved my breath, for the Board was new since the last election, an' there they sat, the damned deevidend-huntin' ship-chandlers, deaf as the adders o' Scripture.

'"We must keep faith wi' the public," said young Steiner.

'"Keep faith wi' the *Breslau*, then,"' I said. '"She's served you well, an' your father before you. She'll need her bottom restiffenin', an' new bed-plates, an' turnin' out the forward boilers, an' re-bor' all three cylinders, an' refacin' all guides, to begin with. It's a three months' job."

'"Because one employee is afraid?" says young Steiner. "Maybe a piano in the Chief Engineer's cabin would be more to the point."

'I crushed my cap in my hands, an' thanked God we'd no bairns an' a bit put by.

'"Understand, gentlemen," I said. "If the *Breslau* is made a sixteen-day boat, ye'll find another engineer."

'"Bannister makes no objection,"' said Holdock.

'"I'm speakin' for myself,"' I said. '"Bannister has bairns." An' then I lost my temper. "Ye can run her into Hell an' out again if ye pay pilotage," I said, "but ye run without me."

'"That's insolence," said young Steiner.

'"At your pleasure," I said, turnin' to go.

'"Ye can consider yourself dismissed. We must preserve discipline among our employees," said old Holdock, an' he looked round to see that the Board was with him. They knew nothin'— God forgie 'em—an' they nodded me oot o' the line after twenty years—after twenty years.

'I went out an' sat down by the hall porter to get my wits again. I'm thinkin' I swore at the Board. Then auld McRimmon—o' McNaughten & McRimmon—came oot o' his office, that's on the same floor, an' looked at me, proppin' up one eyelid wi' his forefinger. Ye know they call him the Blind Deevil, forbye he onythin' but blind, an' no deevil in his dealin's wi' me—McRimmon o' the Black Bird Line.

'"What's here, Mister McPhee?" said he.

'I was past prayin' for by then. "A Chief Engineer sacked after twenty years' service because he'll not risk the *Breslau* on the new timin', an' be damned to ye, McRimmon," I said.

'The auld man sucked in his lips an' whistled. "Ah," said he, "the new timin'. I see!" He doddered into the Board-room I'd just left, an' the Dandie-dog that is just his blind man's leader stayed wi' me. That was providential. In a minute he was back again. "Ye've cast your bread on the watter, McPhee, an' be damned to you," he says. "Whaur's my dog? My word, is he on your knee? There's more discernment in a dog than a Jew. What garred ye curse your

Board, McPhee? It's expensive."

"'They'll pay more for the *Breslau*,' I said. 'Get off my knee, ye smotherin' beastie.'"

"'Bearin's hot, eh?' said McRimmon. 'It's thirty year since a man daur curse me to my face. Time was I'd ha' cast ye doon the stairway for that.'"

"'Forgie's all!' I said. He was wearin' to eighty, as I knew. 'I was wrong, McRimmon; but when a man's shown the door for doin' his plain duty he's not always ceevil.'

"'So I hear,' says McRimmon. 'Ha' ye ony objection to a tramp freighter? It's only fifteen a month, but they say the Blind Deevil feeds a man better than others. She's my *Kite*. Come ben. Ye can thank Dandie, here. I'm no used to thanks. An' noo,' says he, 'what possessed ye to throw up your berth wi' Holdock?'

"'The new timin',' said I. 'The *Breslau* will not stand it.'"

"'Hoot, oot,' said he. 'Ye might ha' crammed her a little— enough to show ye were drivin' her—an' brought her in twa days behind. What's easier than to say ye slowed for bearin's, eh? All my men do it, and—I believe 'em.'"

"'McRimmon,' says I, 'what's her virginity to a lassie?'

'He puckered his dry face an' twisted in his chair. 'The warld an' a',' says he. 'My God, the vara warld an' a'! But what ha' you or me to do wi' virginity, this late along?'

"'This,' I said. 'There's just one thing that each one of us in his trade or profession will not do for ony consideration whatever. If I run to time I run to time, barrin' always the risks o' the high seas. Less than that, under God, I have not done. More than that, by God, I will not do! There's no trick o' the trade I'm not acquaint wi'—'

"'So I've heard,' says McRimmon, dry as a biscuit.

"'But yon matter o' fair rennin's just my Shekinah, ye'll understand. I daurna tamper wi' that. Nursing weak engines is fair craftsmanship; but what the Board ask is cheatin', wi' the risk o' manslaughter addeetional. Ye'll note I know my business."

'There was some more talk, an' next week I went aboard the *Kite*, twenty-five hunder ton, simple compound, a Black Bird tramp. The deeper she rode, the better she'd steam. I've snapped as much as nine out of her, but eight point three was her fair normal. Good food forward an' better aft, all indents passed wi'out marginal remarks, the best coal, new donkeys, and good crews. There was nothin' the old man would not do, except paint. That was his deeficulty. Ye could no more draw paint than his last teeth from him. He'd come down to dock, an' his boats a scandal all along the watter, an' he'd whine an' cry an' say they looked all he could desire. Every owner has his non plus ultra, I've obsairved. Paint was McRimmon's. But you could get round his engines without riskin' your life, an', for all his blindness, I've seen him reject five flawed intermediates, one after the other, on a nod from me; an' his cattle-fittin's were guaranteed for North Atlantic winter weather. Ye ken what that means? McRimmon an' the Black Bird Line, God bless him!

'Oh, I forgot to say she would lie down an' fill her forward deck green, an' snore away into a twenty-knot gale forty-five to the minute, three an' a half knots an hour, the engines runnin' sweet an' true as a bairn breathin' in its sleep. Bell was skipper; an' forbye there's no love lost between crews an' owners, we were fond o' the auld Blind Deevil an' his dog, an' I'm thinkin' he liked us. He was worth the windy side o' twa million sterlin', an' no friend to his own blood-kin. Money's an awfu' thing—overmuch—for a lonely man.

'I'd taken her out twice, there an' back again, when word came o' the *Breslau's* breakdown, just as I prophesied. Calder was her engineer—he's not fit to run a tug down the Solent—and he fairly lifted the engines off the bed-plates, an' they fell down in heaps, by what I heard. So she filled from the after stuffin'-box to the after bulkhead, an' lay star-gazing, with seventy-nine squealin' passengers in the saloon, till the *Camaralzaman* o' Ramsey & Gold's Cartagena line gave her a tow to the tune o' five thousand seven hunder an' forty pound, wi' costs in the Admiralty Court. She was helpless, ye'll understand, an' in no case to meet ony weather. Five thousand seven hunder an' forty pounds, with costs, an' exclusive o' new engines! They'd ha' done better to ha' kept me—on the old timin'.

'But, even so, the new Board were all for retrenchment. Young Steiner, the Jew, was at the bottom of it. They sacked men right an' left, that would not eat the dirt the Board gave 'em. They cut down repairs; they fed crews wi' leavin's an' scrapin's; and, reversin' McRimmon's practice, they hid their defeeciencies wi' paint an' cheap gildin'. Quem Deus vult perrdere prrius dementat, ye remember.

'In January we went to dry-dock, an' in the next dock lay the *Grotkau*, their big freighter that was the Dolabella o' Piegan, Piegan & Walsh's line in '84—a Clyde-built iron boat, a flat-bottomed, pigeon-breasted, under-engined, bull-nosed bitch of a five thousand ton freighter, that would neither steer, nor steam, nor stop when ye asked her. Whiles she'd attend to her helm, whiles she'd take charge, whiles she'd wait to scratch herself, an' whiles she'd buttock into a dockhead. But Holdock and Steiner had bought her cheap, and painted her all over like the Hoor o' Babylon, an' we called her the Hoor for short.' (By the way, McPhee kept to that name throughout the rest of his tale; so you must read accordingly.) 'I went to see young Bannister—he had to take what the Board gave him, an' he an' Calder were shifted together from the *Breslau* to this abortion—an' talkin' to him I went into the dock under her. Her plates were pitted till the men that were paint, paint, paintin' her laughed at it. But the warst was at the last. She'd a great clumsy iron twelve-foot Thresher propeller—Aitcheson designed the *Kite's*—and just on the tail o' the shaft, behind the boss, was a red weepin' crack ye could ha' put a penknife to. Man, it was an awful crack!

"'When d'ye ship a new tail-shaft?' I said to Bannister.

'He knew what I meant. "Oh, yon's a superfeecial flaw," says he, not lookin' at me.

"'Superfeecial Gehenna!' I said. 'Ye'll not take her oot wi' a solution o' continuity that like.'"

"'They'll putty it up this evening,' he said. 'I'm a married man, an'—ye used to know the Board.'

'I e'en said what was gied me in that hour. Ye know how a dry-dock echoes. I saw young Steiner standin' listenin' above me, an', man, he used language provocative of a breach o' the peace. I was a spy and a disgraced employee, an' a corrupter o' young Bannister's morals, an' he'd prosecute me for libel. He went away when I ran up the steps—I'd ha' thrown him into the dock if I'd caught him—an' there I met McRimmon, wi' Dandie pullin' on the chain, guidin' the auld man among the railway lines.

"'McPhee,' said he, 'ye're no paid to fight Holdock, Steiner, Chase & Company, Limited, when ye meet. What's wrong between you?'

"'No more than a tail-shaft rotten as a kail-stump. For ony sakes go an' look, McRimmon. It's a comedietta.'

"'I'm feared o' yon conversational Hebrew,' said he. 'Whaur's the flaw, an' what like?'

"'A seven-inch crack just behind the boss. There's no power on earth will fend it just jarrin' off.'

"'When?'

"'That's beyon' my knowledge,' I said.

"'So it is; so it is,' said McRimmon. 'We've all oor leemitations. Ye're certain it was a crack?'

"'Man, it's a crevasse,' I said, for there were no words to describe the magnitude of it. 'An' young Bannister's sayin' it's no more than a superfeecial flaw!'

"'Weel, I tak' it oor business is to mind oor business. If ye've ony friends aboard her, McPhee, why not bid them to a bit dinner at Radley's?"

"'I was thinkin' o' tea in the cuddy," I said. "Engineers o' tramp freighters cannot afford hotel prices."

"'Na! na!' says the auld man, whimperin'. "Not the cuddy. They'll laugh at my *Kite*, for she's no plastered with paint like the Hoor. Bid them to Radley's, McPhee, an' send me the bill. Thank Dandie, here, man. I'm no used to thanks." Then he turned him round. (I was just thinkin' the vara same thing.) "Mister McPhee," said he, "this is not senile dementia."

"'Preserve 's!" I said, clean jumped oot o' mysel'. "I was but thinkin' you're fey, McRimmon."

'Dod, the auld deevil laughed till he nigh sat down on Dandie. "Send me the bill," says he. "I'm long past champagne, but tell me how it tastes the morn."

'Bell and I bid young Bannister and Calder to dinner at Radley's. They'll have no laughin' an' singin' there, but we took a private room—like yacht-owners fra' Cowes.'

McPhee grinned all over, and lay back to think.

'And then?' said I.

'We were no drunk in ony preceese sense o' the word, but Radley's showed me the dead men. There were six magnums o' dry champagne an' maybe a bottle o' whisky.'

'Do you mean to tell me that you four got away with a magnum and a half a piece, besides whisky?' I demanded.

McPhee looked down upon me from between his shoulders with toleration.

'Man, we were not settin' down to drink,' he said. 'They no more than made us wutty. To be sure, young Bannister laid his head on the table an' greeted like a bairn, an' Calder was all for callin' on Steiner at two in the morn an' painting him galley-green; but they'd been drinkin' the afternoon. Lord, how they twa cursed the Board, an' the *Grotkau*, an' the tail-shaft, an' the engines, an' a'! They didna talk o' superfeecial flaws that night. I mind young Bannister an' Calder shakin' hands on a bond to be revenged on the Board at ony reasonable cost this side o' losing their certificates. Now mark ye how false economy ruins business. The Board fed them like swine (I have good reason to know it), an' I've obsairved wi' my ain people that if ye touch his stomach ye wauken the deil in a Scot. Men will tak' a dredger across the Atlantic if they're well fed, an' fetch her somewhere on the broadside o' the Americas; but bad food's bad service the warld over.

'The bill went to McRimmon, an' he said no more to me till the week-end, when I was at him for more paint, for we'd heard the *Kite* was chartered Liverpool-side. "Bide whaur ye're put," said the Blind Deevil. "Man, do ye wash in champagne? The *Kite's* no leavin' here till I gie the order, an'—how am I to waste paint on her, wi' the *Lammergeyer* docked for who knows how long an' a'?"

'She was our big freighter—McIntyre was engineer—an' I knew she'd come from overhaul not three months. That morn I met McRimmon's head-clerk—ye'll not know him—fair bitin' his nails off wi' mortification.

'"The auld man's gone gyte," says he. "He's withdrawn the *Lammergeyer*."

'"Maybe he has reasons," says I.

'"Reasons! He's daft!"

'"He'll no be daft till he begins to paint," I said.

'"That's just what he's done—and South American freights higher than we'll live to see them again. He's laid her up to paint her—to paint her—to paint her!" says the little clerk, dancin' like a hen on a hot plate. "Five thousand ton o' potential freight rottin' in dry-dock, man; an' he dolin' the paint out in quarter-pound tins, for it cuts him to the heart, mad though he is. An' the *Grotkau*—the *Grotkau* of all conceivable bottoms—soaking up every pound that should be ours at Liverpool!"

'I was staggered wi' this folly—considerin' the dinner at

Radley's in connection wi' the same.

"'Ye may well stare, McPhee," says the head-clerk. "There's engines, an' rollin' stock, an' iron bridges—d'ye know what freights are noo?—an' pianos, an' millinery, an' fancy Brazil cargo o' every species pourin' into the *Grotkau*—the *Grotkau* o' the Jerusalem firm—and the *Lammergeyer's* bein' painted!"

'Losh, I thought he'd drop dead wi' the fits.

'I could say no more than "Obey orders, if ye break owners," but on the *Kite* we believed McRimmon was mad; an' McIntyre of the *Lammergeyer* was for lockin' him up by some patent legal process he'd found in a book o' maritime law. An' a' that week South American freights rose an' rose. It was sinfu'!

'Syne Bell got orders to tak' the *Kite* round to Liverpool in water-ballast, and McRimmon came to bid's good-bye, yammerin' an' whinin' o'er the acres o' paint he'd lavished on the *Lammergeyer*.

"'I look to you to retrieve it," says he. "I look to you to reimburse me!' Fore God, why are ye not cast off? Are ye dawdlin' in dock for a purpose?"

"'What odds, McRimmon?" says Bell. "We'll be a day behind the fair at Liverpool. The *Grotkau's* got all the freight that might ha' been ours an' the *Lammergeyer's*.'" McRimmon laughed an' chuckled—the pairfect eemage o' senile dementia. Ye ken his eyebrows wark up an' down like a gorilla's.

"'Ye're under sealed orders," said he, tee-heein' an' scratchin' himself. "Yon's they"—to be opened seriatim.

'Says Bell, shufflin' the envelopes when the auld man had gone ashore: "We're to creep round a' the south coast, standin' in for orders—this weather, too. There's no question o' his lunacy now."

'Well, we buttocked the auld *Kite* along—vara bad weather we made—standin' in all alongside for telegraphic orders, which are the curse o' skippers. Syne we made over to Holyhead, an' Bell opened the last envelope for the last instructions. I was wi' him in the cuddy, an' he threw it over to me, cryin': "Did ye ever know the like, Mac?"

'I'll no say what McRimmon had written, but he was far from mad. There was a sou'wester brewin' when we made the mouth o' the Mersey, a bitter cold morn wi' a grey-green sea and a grey-green sky—Liverpool weather, as they say; an' there we lay choppin', an' the crew swore. Ye canna keep secrets aboard ship. They thought McRimmon was mad, too.

'Syne we saw the *Grotkau* rollin' oot on the top o' flood, deep an' double deep, wi' her new-painted funnel an' her new-painted boats an' a'. She looked her name, an', moreover, she coughed like it. Calder tauld me at Radley's what ailed his engines, but my own ear would ha' told me twa mile awa', by the beat o' them. Round we came, plungin' an' squatterin' in her wake, an' the wind cut wi' good promise o' more to come. By six it blew hard but clear, an' before the middle watch it was a sou'wester in airnest.

'"She'll edge into Ireland, this gait," says Bell. I was with him on the bridge, watchin' the *Grotkau's* port light. Ye canna see green so far as red, or we'd ha' kept to leeward. We'd no passengers to consider, an' (all eyes being on the *Grotkau*) we fair walked into a liner rampin' home to Liverpool. Or, to be preceese, Bell no more than twisted the *Kite* oot from under her bows, and there was a little damnin' betwix' the twa bridges. Noo a passenger'— McPhee regarded me benignantly—'wad ha' told the papers that as soon as he got to the Customs. We stuck to the *Grotkau's* tail that night an' the next twa days—she slowed down to five knot by my reckonin'—and we lapped along the weary way to the Fastnet.'

'But you don't go by the Fastnet to get to any South American port, do you?' I said.

'We do not. We prefer to go as direct as may be. But we were followin' the *Grotkau*, an' she'd no walk into that gale for ony consideration. Knowin' what I did to her discredit, I couldna blame young Bannister. It was warkin' up to a North Atlantic winter gale, snow an' sleet an' a perishin' wind. Eh, it was like the Deil walkin' abroad o' the surface o' the deep, whuppin' off the top o' the waves before he made up his mind. They'd bore up against it so far, but the minute she was clear o' the Skelligs she fair tucked up her skirts an' ran for it by Dunmore Head. Wow, she rolled!

'"She'll be makin' Smerwick,"' says Bell.

'"She'd ha' tried for Ventry by noo if she meant that,"' I said.

'"They'll roll the funnel oot o' her, this gait,"' says Bell. '"Why canna Bannister keep her head to sea?"'

'"It's the tail-shaft. Ony rollins better than pitchin' wi' superfeecial cracks in the tail-shaft. Calder knows that much," I said.

'"It's ill wark retreevin' steamers this weather," said Bell. His beard and whiskers were frozen to his oilskin, an' the spray was white on the weather side of him. Pairfect North Atlantic winter weather!

'One by one the sea raxed away our three boats, an' the davits were crumpled like ram's horns.

'"Yon's bad," said Bell, at the last. "Ye canna pass a hawser wi' oot a boat." Bell was a vara judeecious man—for an Aberdonian.

'I'm not one that fashes himself for eventualities outside the engine-room, so I e'en slipped down betwixt waves to see how the *Kite* fared. Man, she's the best geared boat of her class that ever left Clyde! Kinloch, my second, knew her as well as I did. I found him dryin' his socks on the main-steam, an' combin' his whiskers wi' the comb Janet gied me last year, for the warld an' a' as though we were in port. I tried the feed, speered into the stoke-hole, thumbed all bearin's, spat on the thrust for luck, gied 'em my blessin', an' took Kinloch's socks before I went up to the bridge again.

'Then Bell handed me the wheel, an' went below to warm himself. When he came up my gloves were frozen to the spokes an' the ice clicked over my eyelids. Pairfect North Atlantic winter weather, as I was sayin'.

'The gale blew out by night, but we lay in smotherin' cross-seas that made the auld *Kite* chatter from stem to stern. I slowed to thirty-four, I mind—no, thirty-seven. There was a long swell the morn, an' the *Grotkau* was headin' into it west awa'.

"'She'll win to Rio yet, tail-shaft or no tail-shaft,'" says Bell.

"'Last night shook her," I said. "She'll jar it off yet, mark my word."

'We were then, maybe, a hunder and fifty mile west-sou'west o' Slyne Head, by dead reckonin'. Next day we made a hunder an' thirty—ye'll note we were not racin' boats—an' the day after a hunder an' sixty-one, an' that made us, we'll say, Eighteen an' a bittock west, an' maybe Fifty-one an' a bittock north, crossin' all the North Atlantic liner lanes on the long slant, always in sight o' the *Grotkau*, creepin' up by night and fallin' awa' by day. After the gale it was cold weather wi' dark nights.

'I was in the engine-room on Friday night, just before the middle watch, when Bell whustled down the tube: "She's done it;" an' up I came.

'The *Grotkau* was just a fair distance south, an' one by one she ran up the three red lights in a vertical line—the sign of a steamer not under control.

"'Yon's a tow for us," said Bell, lickin' his chops. "She'll be worth more than the *Breslau*. We'll go down to her, McPhee!"

"'Bide a while," I said. "The seas fair throng wi' ships here."

"'Reason why," said Bell. "It's a fortune gaun beggin'. What d'ye think, man?"

"'Gie her till daylight. She knows we're here. If Bannister needs help he'll loose a rocket."

"'Wha told ye Bannister's need? We'll ha' some rag-an'-bone tramp snappin' her up under oor nose," said he; an' he put the wheel over. We were goin' slow.

"'Bannister wad like better to go home on a liner an' eat in the saloon. Mind ye what they said o' Holdock & Steiner's food that night at Radley's? Keep her awa', man—keep her awa'. A tow's a tow, but a derelict's big salvage."

"'E-eh!' said Bell. "Yon's an inshot o' yours, Mac. I love ye like a brother. We'll bide whaur we are till daylight;" an' he kept her awa'.

'Syne up went a rocket forward, an' twa on the bridge, an' a blue light aft. Syne a tar-barrel forward again.

"'She's sinkin'," said Bell. "It's all gaun, an' I'll get no more than a pair o' night-glasses for pickin' up young Bannister—the fool!"

"'Fair an' soft again," I said. "She's signallin' to the south of us. Bannister knows as well as I that one rocket would bring the *Breslau*. He'll no be wastin' fireworks for nothin'. Hear her ca'!"

'The *Grotkau* whustled an' whustled for five minutes, an' then there were more fireworks—a regular exhibeetion.

"'That's no for men in the regular trade," says Bell. "Ye're right, Mac. That's for a cuddy full o' passengers." He blinked through the night-glasses when it lay a bit thick to southward.

"'What d'ye make of it?" I said.

"'Liner," he says. "Yon's her rocket. Ou, ay; they've waukened the gold-strapped skipper, an'—noo they've waukened the passengers. They're turnin' on the electrics, cabin by cabin. Yon's anither rocket! They're comin' up to help the perishin' in deep watters."

"'Gie me the glass," I said.

But Bell danced on the bridge, clean dementit. "Mails—mails—mails!" said he. "Under contract wi' the Government for the due conveyance o' the mails; an' as such, Mac, ye'll note, she may rescue life at sea, but she canna tow!—she canna tow! Yon's her night-signal. She'll be up in half an hour!"

"'Gowk!" I said, "an' we blazin' here wi' all oor lights. Oh, Bell, ye're a fool!"

'He tumbled off the bridge forward, an' I tumbled aft, an' before ye could wink our lights were oot, the engine-room hatch was covered, an' we lay pitch-dark, watchin' the lights o' the liner come up that the *Grotkau*'d been signallin' to. Twenty knot an hour she came, every cabin lighted, an' her boats swung awa'. It was grandly done, an' in the inside of an hour. She stopped like Mrs Holdock's machine; down went the gangway, down went the boats, an' in ten minutes we heard the passengers cheerin', an' awa' she fled.

'"They'll tell o' this all the days they live," said Bell. "A rescue at sea by night, as pretty as a play. Young Bannister an' Calder will be drinkin' in the saloon, an' six months hence the Board o' Trade 'll gie the skipper a pair o' binoculars. It's vara philanthropic all round."

'We'll lay by till day—ye may think we waited for it wi' sore eyes an' there sat the *Grotkau*, her nose a bit cocked, just leerin' at us. She looked pairfectly ridiculous.

'"She'll be fillin' aft," says Bell; "for why is she down by the stern? The tail-shaft's punched a hole in her, an'—we 've no boats. There's three hunder thousand pound sterlin', at a conservative estimate, droonin' before our eyes. What's to do?" An' his bearin's got hot again in a minute; for he was an incontinent man.

'"Run her as near as ye daur," I said. "Gie me a jacket an' a lifeline, an' I'll swum for it." There was a bit lump of a sea, an' it was cold in the wind—vara cold; but they'd gone overside like passengers, young Bannister an' Calder an' a', leaving the gangway down on the lee-side. It would ha' been a flyin' in the face o' manifest Providence to overlook the invitation. We were within fifty yards o' her while Kinloch was garmin' me all over wi' oil behind the galley; an' as we ran past I went outboard for the salvage o' three hunder thousand pound. Man, it was perishin' cold, but I'd done my job judgmatically, an' came scrapin' all along her side slap on to the lower gratin' o' the gangway. No one more astonished than me, I assure ye. Before I'd caught my breath I'd skinned both my knees on the gratin', an' was climbin' up before she rolled again. I made my line fast to the rail, an' squattered aft to young Bannister's cabin, whaaur I dried me wi' everything in his bunk, an' put on every conceivable sort o' rig I found till the blood was circulatin'. Three pair drawers, I mind I found—to begin upon—an' I needed them all. It was the coldest cold I remember in all my experience.

'Syne I went aft to the engine-room. The *Grotkau* sat on her own tail, as they say. She was vara shortshafted, an' her gear was all aft. There was four or five foot o' water in the engine-room slummockin' to and fro, black an' greasy; maybe there was six foot. The stoke-hold doors were screwed home, an' the stoke-hold was tight enough, but for a minute the mess in the engine-room deceived me. Only for a minute, though, an' that was because I was not, in a manner o' speakin', as calm as ordinar'. I looked again to mak' sure. 'T was just black wi' bilge: dead watter that must ha' come in fortuitously, ye ken.'

'McPhee, I'm only a passenger,' I said, 'but you don't persuade me that six foot o' water can come into an engine-room fortuitously.'

'Wha's tryin' to persuade one way or the other?' McPhee retorted. 'I'm statin' the facts o' the case—the simple, natural facts. Six or seven foot o' dead watter in the engine-room is a vara depressin' sight if ye think there's like to be more comin'; but I did not consider that such was likely, and so, ye'll note, I was not depressed.'

'That's all very well, but I want to know about the water,' I said.

'I've told ye. There was six feet or more there, wi' Calder's cap floatin' on top.'

'Where did it come from?'

'Weel, in the confusion o' things after the propeller had dropped off an' the engines were racin' an' a', it's vara possible that Calder might ha' lost it off his head an' no troubled himself to pick it up again. I remember seein' that cap on him at Southampton.'

'I don't want to know about the cap. I'm asking where the water came from and what it was doing there, and why you were so certain that it wasn't a leak, McPhee?'

'For good reason—for good an' sufficient reason.'

'Give it to me, then.'

'Weel, it's a reason that does not properly concern myself only. To be preceese, I'm of opinion that it was due, the watter, in part to an error o' judgment in another man. We can a' mak' mistakes.'

'Oh, I beg your pardon?'

'I got me to the rail again, an', "What's wrang?" said Bell, hailin'.

'"She'll do," I said. "Send's o'er a hawser, an' a man to steer. I'll pull him in by the life-line."

'I could see heads bobbin' back an' forth, an' a whuff or two o' strong words. Then Bell said, "They'll not trust themselves—one of 'em—in this waiter—except Kinloch, an' I'll no spare him."

'"The more salvage to me, then," I said. "I'll make shift solo."

'Says one dock-rat, at this: "D'ye think she's safe?"

'"I'll guarantee ye nothing," I said, "except maybe a hammerin' for keepin' me this long."

'Then he sings out: "There's no more than one life-belt, an' they canna find it, or I'd come."

'"Throw him over, the Jezebel," I said, for I was oot o' patience; an' they took haud o' that volunteer before he knew what was in store, and hove him over, in the bight of my life-line. So I e'en hauled him upon the sag of it, hand-over-fist—a vara welcome recruit when I'd tilted the salt watter oot of him; for, by the way, he could na swim.

'Syne they bent a twa-inch rope to the life-line, an' a hawser to that, an' I led the rope o'er the drum of a hand-winch forward, an' we sweated the hawser inboard an' made it fast to the *Grotkau's* bitts.

'Bell brought the *Kite* so close I feared she'd roll in an' do the *Grotkau's* plates a mischief. He hove anither life-line to me, an' went astern, an' we had all the weary winch-work to do again wi' a second hawser. For all that, Bell was right: we'd a long tow before us, an' though Providence had helped us that far, there was no sense in leavin' too much to its keepin'. When the second hawser was fast, I was wet wi' sweat, an' I cried Bell to tak' up his slack an' go home. The other man was by way o' helpin' the work wi' askin' for drinks, but I e'en told him he must hand reef an' steer, beginnin' with steerin', for I was goin' to turn in. He steered—oh, ay, he steered, in a manner o' speakin'. At the least, he grippit the spokes an' twiddled 'em an' looked wise, but I doubt if the Hoor ever felt it. I turned in there an' then, to young Bannister's bunk, an' slept past expression. I waukened ragin' wi' hunger, a fair lump o' sea runnin', the *Kite* snorin' awa' four knots an hour; an' the *Grotkau* slappin' her nose under, an' yawin' an' standin' over at discretion. She was a most disgracefu' tow. But the shameful thing of all was the food. I raxed me a meal fra galley-shelves an' pantries an' lazareetes an' cubby-holes that I would not ha' gied to the mate of a Cardiff collier; an' ye ken we say a Cardiff mate will eat clinkers to save waste. I'm sayin' it was simply vile! The crew had written what they thought of it on the new paint o' the fo'c'sle, but I had not a decent soul wi' me to complain on. There was nothin' for me to do save watch the hawsers an' the *Kite's* tail squatterin' down in white watter when she lifted to a sea; so I got steam on the after donkey-pump, an' pumped oot the engine-room. There's no sense in leavin' watter loose in a ship. When she was dry, I went doun the shaft-tunnel, an' found she was leakin' a little through the stuffin'-box, but nothin' to make wark. The propeller had e'en jarred off, as I knew it must, an' Calder had been waitin' for it to go wi' his hand on the gear. He told me as much when I met him ashore. There was nothin' started or strained. It had just slipped awa' to the bed o' the Atlantic as easy as a man dyin' wi' due warning—a most providential business for all concerned. Syne I took stock o' the *Grotkau's* upper works. Her boats had been smashed on the davits, an' here an' there was the rail missin', an' a ventilator or two had fetched awa', an' the bridge-rails were bent by the seas; but her hatches were tight, and she'd taken no sort of harm. Dod, I came to hate her like a human bein', for I was eight weary days aboard, starvin'—ay, starvin'—within a cable's length o' plenty. All day I laid in the bunk reading *A Woman-Hater*, the grandest book Charlie Reade ever wrote, an' pickin' a toothful here an' there. It was weary, weary work. Eight days, man, I was aboard the *Grotkau*, an' not one full meal did I make. Sma' blame her crew would not stay by her. The other man? Oh I warked him wi' a vengeance to keep him warm.

'It came on to blow when we fetched soundin's, an' that kept me standin' by the hawsers, lashed to the capstan, breathin' twixt green seas. I near died o' cauld an' hunger, for the *Grotkau* towed like a barge, an' Bell howkit her along through or over. It was vara thick up-Channel, too. We were standin' in to make some sort o' light, an' we near walked over twa three fishin'-boats, an' they cried us we were ov'er close to Falmouth. Then we were near cut down by a drunken foreign fruiter that was blunderin' between us an' the shore, and it got thicker an' thicker that night, an' I could feel by the tow Bell did not know whaur he was. Losh, we knew in the morn, for the wind blew the fog oot like a candle, an' the sun came clear; and as surely as McRimmon gied me my cheque, the shadow o' the Eddystone lay across our tow-rope! We were that near—ay, we were that near! Bell fetched the *Kite* round with the jerk that came close to tearin' the bitts out o' the *Grotkau*, an' I mind I thanked my Maker in young Bannister's cabin when we were inside Plymouth breakwater.

'The first to come aboard was McRimmon, wi' Dandie. Did I tell you our orders were to take anything we found into Plymouth? The auld deil had just come down overnight, puttin' two an' two together from what Calder had told him when the liner landed the *Grotkau's* men. He had preceesely hit oor time. I'd hailed Bell for something to eat, an' he sent it o'er in the same boat wi' McRimmon, when the auld man came to me. He grinned an' slapped his legs and worked his eyebrows the while I ate.

"'How do Holdock, Steiner & Chase feed their men?'" said he.

"'Ye can see,' I said, knockin' the top off another beer-bottle. "I did not sign to be starved, McRimmon."

"'Nor to swum, either,' said he, for Bell had tauld him how I carried the line aboard. "Well, I'm thinkin' you'll be no loser. What freight could we ha' put into the *Lammergeyer* would equal salvage on four hunder thousand pounds—hull an' cargo? Eh, McPhee? This cuts the liver out o' Holdock, Steiner, Chase & Company, Limited. Eh, McPhee? An' I'm sufferin' from senile dementia now? Eh, McPhee? An' I'm not daft, am I, till I begin to paint the *Lammergeyer*? Eh, McPhee? Ye may weel lift your leg, Dandie! I ha' the laugh o' them all. Ye found watter in the engine-room?"

"'To speak wi'oot prejudice,' I said, "there was some watter."

"'They thought she was sinkin' after the propeller went. She filled wi' extraordinary rapeedity. Calder said it grieved him an' Bannister to abandon her."

'I thought o' the dinner at Radley's, an' what like o' food I'd eaten for eight days.

"'It would grieve them sore,' I said.

"'But the crew would not hear o' stayin' and taking their chances. They're gaun up an' down sayin' they'd ha' starved first.'

"'They'd ha' starved if they'd stayed,' said I.

"'I tak' it, fra Calder's account, there was a mutiny a'most.'

"'Ye know more than I, McRimmon,' I said. "Speakin' wi'oot prejudice, for we're all in the same boat, who opened the bilge-cock?"

"'Oh, that's it—is it?' said the auld man, an' I could see he was surprised. "A bilge-cock, ye say?"

'"I believe it was a bilge-cock. They were all shut when I came aboard, but some one had flooded the engine-room eight feet over all, and shut it off with the worm-an'-wheel gear from the second gratin' afterwards."

'"Losh!" said McRimmon. "The ineequity o' man's beyond belief. But it's awfu' discreditable to Holdock, Steiner & Chase, if that came oot in court."

'"It's just my own curiosity," I said.

'"Aweel, Dandie's afflicted wi' the same disease. Dandie, strive against curiosity, for it brings a little dog into traps an' suchlike. Whaur was the *Kite* when yon painted liner took off the *Grotkau's* people?"

'"Just there or thereabouts," I said.

'"An' which o' you twa thought to cover your lights?" said he, winkin'.

'"Dandie," I said to the dog, "we must both strive against curiosity. It's an unremunerative business. What's our chance o' salvage, Dandie?"

'He laughed till he choked. "Tak' what I gie you, McPhee, an' be content," he said. "Lord, how a man wastes time when he gets old. Get aboard the *Kite*, mon, as soon as ye can. I've clean forgot there's a Baltic charter yammerin' for you at London. That'll be your last voyage, I'm thinkin', excep' by way o' pleasure."

'Steiner's men were comin' aboard to take charge an' tow her round, an' I passed young Steiner in a boat as I went to the *Kite*. He looked down his nose; but McRimmon pipes up: "Here's the man ye owe the *Grotkau* to—at a price, Steiner—at a price! Let me introduce Mr McPhee to you. Maybe ye've met before; but ye've vara little luck in keepin' your men—ashore or afloat!"

'Young Steiner looked angry enough to eat him as he chuckled an' whustled in his dry old throat.

'"Ye've not got your award yet," Steiner says.

'"Na, na," says the auld man, in a screech ye could hear to the

Hoe, "but I've twa million sterlin', an' no bairns, ye Judeeas Apella, if ye mean to fight; an' I'll match ye p'und for p'und till the last p'und's oot. Ye ken me, Steiner! I'm McRimmon o' McNaughten & McRimmon!"

'"Dod," he said betwix' his teeth, sittin' back in the boat, "I've waited fourteen year to break that Jew-firm, an' God be thankit I'll do it now."

'The *Kite* was in the Baltic while the auld man was warkin' his warks, but I know the assessors valued the *Grotkau*, all told, at over three hunder and sixty thousand—her manifest was a treat o' richness—an' McRimmon got a third for salvin' an abandoned ship. Ye see, there's vast deeference between towin' a ship wi' men on her an' pickin' up a derelict—a vast deeference—in pounds sterlin'. Moreover, twa three o' the *Grotkau's* crew were burnin' to testify about food, an' there was a note o' Calder to the Board, in regard to the tail-shaft, that would ha' been vara damagin' if it had come into court. They knew better than to fight.

'Syne the *Kite* came back, an' McRimmon paid off me an' Bell personally, an' the rest of the crew pro rata, I believe it's ca'ed. My share—oor share, I should say—was just twenty-five thousand pound sterlin'.'

At this point Janet jumped up and kissed him.

'Five-and-twenty thousand pound sterlin'. Noo, I'm fra the North, and I'm not the like to fling money awa' rashly, but I'd gie six months' pay—one hunder an' twenty pounds—to know who flooded the engine-room of the *Grotkau*. I'm fairly well acquaint wi' McRimmon's eediosyncrasies, and he'd no hand in it. It was not Calder, for I've asked him, an' he wanted to fight me. It would be in the highest degree unprofessional o' Calder—not fightin', but openin' bilge-cocks—but for a while I thought it was him. Ay, I judged it might be him—under temptation.'

'What's your theory?' I demanded.

'Weel, I'm inclined to think it was one o' those singular

providences that remind us we're in the hands o' Higher Powers.' .

'It couldn't open and shut itself?'

'I did not mean that; but some half-starvin' oiler or, maybe, trimmer must ha' opened it awhile to mak' sure o' leavin' the *Grotkau*. It's a demoralizin' thing to see an engine-room flood up after any accident to the gear—demoralizin' and deceptive both. Aweel, the man got what he wanted, for they went aboard the liner cryin' that the *Grotkau* was sinkin'. But it's curious to think o' the consequences. In a' human probability, he's bein' damned in heaps at the present moment aboard another tramp freighter; an' here am I, wi' five-an'-twenty thousand pounds invested, resolute to go to sea no more—providential's the preceese word—except as a passenger, ye'll understand, Janet.'

McPhee kept his word. He and Janet went for a voyage as passengers in the first-class saloon. They paid seventy pounds for their berths; and Janet found a very sick woman in the second-class saloon, so that for sixteen days she lived below, and chatted with the stewardesses at the foot of the second-saloon stairs while her patient slept. McPhee was a passenger for exactly twenty-four hours. Then the engineers' mess—where the oilcloth tables are—joyfully took him to its bosom, and for the rest of the voyage that company was richer by the unpaid services of a highly certificated engineer.

5

THE FINEST STORY IN THE WORLD

> "Or ever the knightly years were gone
> With the old world to the grave,
> I was a king in Babylon
> And you were a Christian slave,"
> —W.E. Henley.

His name was Charlie Mears; he was the only son of his mother who was a widow, and he lived in the north of London, coming into the City every day to work in a bank. He was twenty years old and suffered from aspirations. I met him in a public billiard-saloon where the marker called him by his given name, and he called the marker 'Bulls-eyes'. Charlie explained, a little nervously, that he had only come to the place to look on, and since looking on at games of skill is not a cheap amusement for the young, I suggested that Charlie should go back to his mother.

That was our first step toward better acquaintance. He would call on me sometimes in the evenings instead of running about London with his fellow-clerks; and before long, speaking of himself as a young man must, he told me of his aspirations, which were all literary. He desired to make himself an undying name chiefly through verse, though he was not above sending stories of love and death to the drop-a-penny-in-the-slot journals. It was my fate to sit still while Charlie read me poems of many hundred lines, and bulky fragments of plays that would surely shake the world. My reward was his unreserved confidence, and the self-revelations and troubles of a young man are almost as holy as those of a maiden. Charlie had never fallen in love, but was anxious to do so on the first opportunity; he believed in all things good and all things honorable, but, at the same time, was curiously careful to let me see that he knew his way about the world as befitted a bank clerk on twenty-five shillings a week. He rhymed 'dove' with 'love' and 'moon' with 'June', and devoutly believed that they had never so been rhymed before. The long lame gaps in his plays he filled up with hasty words of apology and description and swept on, seeing all that he intended to do so clearly that he esteemed it already done, and turned to me for applause.

I fancy that his mother did not encourage his aspirations, and I know that his writing table at home was the edge of his washstand. This he told me almost at the outset of our acquaintance; when he was ravaging my bookshelves, and a little before I was implored to speak the truth as to his chances of 'writing something really great, you know'. Maybe I encouraged him too much, for, one night, he called on me, his eyes flaming with excitement, and said breathlessly:

'Do you mind—can you let me stay here and write all this evening? I won't interrupt you, I won't really. There's no place for me to write in at my mother's.'

'What's the trouble?' I said, knowing well what that trouble was.

'I've a notion in my head that would make the most splendid story that was ever written. Do let me write it out here. It's such a notion!'

There was no resisting the appeal. I set him a table; he hardly thanked me, but plunged into the work at once. For half an hour the pen scratched without stopping. Then Charlie sighed and tugged his hair. The scratching grew slower, there were more erasures, and at last ceased. The finest story in the world would not come forth.

'It looks such awful rot now,' he said, mournfully. 'And yet it seemed so good when I was thinking about it. What's wrong?'

I could not dishearten him by saying the truth. So I answered: 'Perhaps you don't feel in the mood for writing.'

'Yes I do—except when I look at this stuff. Ugh!'

'Read me what you've done,' I said. He read, and it was wondrous bad, and he paused at all the specially turgid sentences, expecting a little approval; for he was proud of those sentences, as I knew he would be.

'It needs compression,' I suggested, cautiously.

'I hate cutting my things down. I don't think you could alter a word here without spoiling the sense. It reads better aloud than when I was writing it.'

'Charlie, you're suffering from an alarming disease afflicting a numerous class. Put the thing by, and tackle it again in a week.'

'I want to do it at once. What do you think of it?'

'How can I judge from a half-written tale? Tell me the story as it lies in your head.'

Charlie told, and in the telling there was everything that his ignorance had so carefully prevented from escaping into the written word. I looked at him, and wondering whether it were possible, that he did not know the originality, the power of the notion that had come in his way? It was distinctly a Notion among notions. Men had been puffed up with pride by notions not a tithe as excellent and practicable. But Charlie babbled on serenely, interrupting the current of pure fancy with samples of horrible sentences that he purposed to use. I heard him out to the end. It would be folly to allow his idea to remain in his own inept hands, when I could do so much with it. Not all that could be done indeed; but, oh so much!

'What do you think?' he said, at last. 'I fancy I shall call it "The Story of a Ship".'

'I think the idea's pretty good; but you won't be able to handle it for ever so long. Now I—'Would it be of any use to you? Would you care to take it? I should be proud,' said Charlie, promptly.

There are few things sweeter in this world than the guileless, hot-headed, intemperate, open admiration of a junior. Even a woman in her blindest devotion does not fall into the gait of the man she adores, tilt her bonnet to the angle at which he wears his hat, or interlard her speech with his pet oaths. And Charlie did all these things. Still it was necessary to salve my conscience before I possessed myself of Charlie's thoughts.

'Let's make a bargain. I'll give you a fiver for the notion,' I said.

Charlie became a bank clerk at once.

'Oh, that's impossible. Between two pals, you know, if I may call you so, and speaking as a man of the world, I couldn't. Take the notion if it's any use to you. I've heaps more.'

He had—none knew this better than I—but they were the notions of other men.

'Look at it as a matter of business—between men of the world,' I returned. 'Five pounds will buy you any number of poetry-books. Business is business, and you may be sure I shouldn't give that price unless—' 'Oh, if you put it that way,' said Charlie, visibly moved by the thought of the books. The bargain was clinched with an agreement that he should at unstated intervals come to me with all the notions that he possessed, should have a table of his own to write at, and unquestioned right to inflict upon me all his poems and fragments of poems. Then I said, 'Now tell me how you came by this idea.'

'It came by itself.' Charlie's eyes opened a little.

'Yes, but you told me a great deal about the hero that you must have read before somewhere.'

'I haven't any time for reading, except when you let me sit

here, and on Sundays I'm on my bicycle or down the river all day. There's nothing wrong about the hero, is there?'

'Tell me again and I shall understand clearly. You say that your hero went pirating. How did he live?'

'He was on the lower deck of this ship-thing that I was telling you about.'

'What sort of ship?'

'It was the kind rowed with oars, and the sea spurts through the oar-holes and the men row sitting up to their knees in water. Then there's a bench running down between the two lines of oars and an overseer with a whip walks up and down the bench to make the men work.'

'How do you know that?'

'It's in the tale. There's a rope running overhead, looped to the upper deck, for the overseer to catch hold of when the ship rolls. When the overseer misses the rope once and falls among the rowers, remember the hero laughs at him and gets licked for it. He's chained to his oar of course—the hero.'

'How is he chained?'

'With an iron band round his waist fixed to the bench he sits on, and a sort of handcuff on his left wrist chaining him to the oar. He's on the lower deck where the worst men are sent, and the only light comes from the hatchways and through the oar-holes. Can't you imagine the sunlight just squeezing through between the handle and the hole and wobbling about as the ship moves?'

'I can, but I can't imagine your imagining it.'

'How could it be any other way? Now you listen to me. The long oars on the upper deck are managed by four men to each bench, the lower ones by three, and the lowest of all by two. Remember it's quite dark on the lowest deck and all the men there go mad. When a man dies at his oar on that deck he isn't thrown overboard, but cut up in his chains and stuffed through the oar-hole in little pieces.'

'Why?' I demanded, amazed, not so much at the information as the tone of command in which it was flung out.

'To save trouble and to frighten the others. It needs two overseers to drag a man's body up to the top deck; and if the men at the lower deck oars were left alone, of course they'd stop rowing and try to pull up the benches by all standing up together in their chains.'

'You've a most provident imagination. Where have you been reading about galleys and galley-slaves?'

'Nowhere that I remember. I row a little when I get the chance. But, perhaps, if you say so, I may have read something.'

He went away shortly afterward to deal with booksellers, and I wondered how a bank clerk aged twenty could put into my hands with a profligate abundance of detail, all given with absolute assurance, the story of extravagant and bloodthirsty adventure, riot, piracy, and death in unnamed seas. He had led his hero a desperate dance through revolt against the overseers, to command of a ship of his own, and ultimate establishment of a kingdom on an island 'somewhere in the sea, you know'; and, delighted with my paltry five pounds, had gone out to buy the notions of other men, that these might teach him how to write. I had the consolation of knowing that this notion was mine by right of purchase, and I thought that I could make something of it.

When next he came to me he was drunk—royally drunk on many poets for the first time revealed to him. His pupils were dilated, his words tumbled over each other, and he wrapped himself in quotations. Most of all was he drunk with Longfellow.

'Isn't it splendid? Isn't it superb?' he cried, after hasty greetings. 'Listen to this—

'"Wouldst thou," so the helmsman answered,
"Know the secret of the sea?
Only those who brave its dangers
Comprehend its mystery."

By gum!

"'Only those who brave its dangers
Comprehend its mystery.'"

He repeated twenty times, walking up and down the room and forgetting me. 'But I can understand it too,' he said to himself. 'I don't know how to thank you for that fiver. And this; listen—

"'I remember the black wharves and the ships
And the sea-tides tossing free,
And the Spanish sailors with bearded lips,
And the beauty and mystery of the ships,
And the magic of the sea."

'I haven't braved any dangers, but I feel as if I knew all about it.'

'You certainly seem to have a grip of the sea. Have you ever seen it?'

'When I was a little chap I went to Brighton once; we used to live in Coventry, though, before we came to London. I never saw it—

"'When descends on the Atlantic
The gigantic
Storm-wind of the Equinox.'"

He shook me by the shoulder to make me understand the passion that was shaking himself.

'When that storm comes,' he continued, 'I think that all the oars in the ship that I was talking about get broken, and the rowers have their chests smashed in by the bucking oar-heads. By the way, have you done anything with that notion of mine yet?'

'No. I was waiting to hear more of it from you. Tell me how in the world you're so certain about the fittings of the ship. You know nothing of ships.'

'I don't know. It's as real as anything to me until I try to write it down. I was thinking about it only last night in bed, after you had loaned me *Treasure Island*; and I made up a a whole lot of new things to go into the story.'

'What sort of things?'

'About the food the men ate; rotten figs and black beans and wine in a skin bag, passed from bench to bench.'

'Was the ship built so long ago as that?'

'As what? I don't know whether it was long ago or not. It's only a notion, but sometimes it seems just as real as if it was true. Do I bother you with talking about it?'

'Not in the least. Did you make up anything else?'

'Yes, but it's nonsense.' Charlie flushed a little.

'Never mind; let's hear about it.'

'Well, I was thinking over the story, and after awhile I got out of bed and wrote down on a piece of paper the sort of stuff the men might be supposed to scratch on their oars with the edges of their handcuffs. It seemed to make the thing more lifelike. It is so real to me, y'know.'

'Have you the paper on you?'

'Ye-es, but what's the use of showing it? It's only a lot of scratches. All the same, we might have 'em reproduced in the book on the front page.'

'I'll attend to those details. Show me what your men wrote.'

He pulled out of his pocket a sheet of note-paper, with a single line of scratches upon it, and I put this carefully away.

'What is it supposed to mean in English?' I said.

'Oh, I don't know. Perhaps it means "I'm beastly tired". It's great nonsense,' he repeated, 'but all those men in the ship seem as real people to me. Do do something to the notion soon; I should like to see it written and printed.'

'But all you've told me would make a long book.'

'Make it then. You've only to sit down and write it out.'

'Give me a little time. Have you any more notions?'

'Not just now. I'm reading all the books I've bought. They're splendid.'

When he had left I looked at the sheet of note-paper with the inscription upon it. Then I took my head tenderly between both hands, to make certain that it was not coming off or turning round. Then...but there seemed to be no interval between quitting my rooms and finding myself arguing with a policeman outside a door marked 'Private' in a corridor of the British Museum. All I demanded, as politely as possible, was 'the Greek antiquity man'. The policeman knew nothing except the rules of the Museum, and it became necessary to forage through all the houses and offices inside the gates. An elderly gentleman called away from his lunch put an end to my search by holding the note-paper between finger and thumb and sniffing at it scornfully.

'What does this mean? H'mm,' said he. 'So far as I can ascertain it is an attempt to write extremely corrupt Greek on the part'—here he glared at me with intention—' of an extremely illiterate—ah—person.' He read slowly from the paper, 'Pollock, Erckman, Tauchnitz, Henniker'—four names familiar to me.

'Can you tell me what the corruption is supposed to mean—the gist of the thing?' I asked.

'I have been—many times—overcome with weariness in this particular employment. That is the meaning.' He returned me the paper, and I fled without a word of thanks, explanation, or apology.

I might have been excused for forgetting much. To me of all men had been given the chance to write the most marvellous tale in the world, nothing less than the story of a Greek galley-slave, as told by himself. Small wonder that his dreaming had seemed real to Charlie. The Fates that are so careful to shut the doors of each successive life behind us had, in this case, been neglectful, and Charlie was looking, though that he did not know, where never man had been permitted to look with full knowledge since Time began. Above all, he was absolutely ignorant of the knowledge sold to me for five pounds; and he would retain that ignorance, for bank clerks do not understand metempsychosis, and a sound commercial education does not include Greek. He would supply m—here I capered among the dumb gods of Egypt and laughed in their battered faces—with material to make my tale sure—so sure that the world would hail it as an impudent and vamped fiction. And I—I alone would know that it was absolutely and literally true. I—I alone held this jewel to my hand for the cutting and polishing. Therefore I danced again among the gods till a policeman saw me and took steps in my direction.

It remained now only to encourage Charlie to talk, and here there was no difficulty. But I had forgotten those accursed books of poetry. He came to me time after time, as useless as a surcharged phonograph—drunk on Byron, Shelley, or Keats. Knowing now what the boy had been in his past lives, and desperately anxious not to lose one word of his babble, I could not hide from him my respect and interest. He misconstrued both into respect for the present soul of Charlie Mears, to whom life was as new as it was to Adam, and interest in his readings; and stretched my patience to breaking point by reciting poetry-not his own now, but that of others. I wished every English poet blotted out of the memory of mankind. I blasphemed the mightiest names of song because they had drawn Charlie from the path of direct narrative, and would, later, spur him to imitate them; but I choked down my impatience until the first flood of enthusiasm should have spent itself and the boy returned to his dreams.

'What's the use of my telling you what I think, when these chaps wrote things for the angels to read?' he growled, one evening. 'Why don't you write something like theirs?'

'I don't think you're treating me quite fairly,' I said, speaking under strong restraint.

'I've given you the story,' he said, shortly replunging into 'Lara'.

'But I want the details.'

'The things I make up about that damned ship that you call a galley? They're quite easy. You can just make 'em up yourself. Turn up the gas a little, I want to go on reading.'

I could have broken the gas globe over his head for his amazing stupidity. I could indeed make up things for myself did I only know what Charlie did not know that he knew. But since the doors were shut behind me I could only wait his youthful pleasure and strive to keep him in good temper. One minute's want of guard might spoil a priceless revelation: now and again he would toss his books aside—he kept them in my rooms, for his mother would have been shocked at the waste of good money had she seen them—and launched into his sea dreams. Again I cursed all the poets of England. The plastic mind of the bank clerk had been overlaid, coloured and distorted by that which he had read, and the result as delivered was a confused tangle of other voices most like the muttered song through a City telephone in the busiest part of the day.

He talked of the galley—his own galley had he but known it—with illustrations borrowed from the 'Bride of Abydos'. He pointed the experiences of his hero with quotations from 'The Corsair', and threw in deep and desperate moral reflections from 'Cain' and 'Manfred', expecting me to use them all. Only when the talk turned on Longfellow were the jarring cross-currents dumb, and I knew that Charlie was speaking the truth as he remembered it.

'What do you think of this?' I said one evening, as soon as I understood the medium in which his memory worked best, and, before he could expostulate read him the whole of 'The Saga of King Olaf'!

He listened open-mouthed, flushed his hands drumming on the back of the sofa where he lay, till I came to the Songs of Einar Tamberskelver and the verse:

'Einar then, the arrow taking

From the loosened string,
Answered: 'That was Norway breaking
'Neath thy hand, O King.'
He gasped with pure delight of sound.

'That's better than Byron, a little,' I ventured.

'Better? Why it's true! How could he have known?'

I went back and repeated:

'"What was that?" said Olaf, standing
On the quarter-deck,
"Something heard I like the stranding
Of a shattered wreck."'

'How could he have known how the ships crash and the oars rip out and go z-zzp all along the line? Why only the other night... But go back please and read "The Skerry of Shrieks" again.'

'No, I'm tired. Let's talk. What happened the other night?'

'I had an awful nightmare about that galley of ours. I dreamed I was drowned in a fight. You see we ran alongside another ship in harbour. The water was dead still except where our oars whipped it up. You know where I always sit in the galley?' He spoke haltingly at first, under a fine English fear of being laughed at.

'No. That's news to me,' I answered, meekly, my heart beginning to beat.

'On the fourth oar from the bow on the right side on the upper deck. There were four of us at that oar, all chained. I remember watching the water and trying to get my handcuffs off before the row began. Then we closed up on the other ship, and all their fighting men jumped over our bulwarks, and my bench broke and I was pinned down with the three other fellows on top of me, and the big oar jammed across our backs.'

'Well?' Charlie's eyes were alive and alight. He was looking at the wall behind my chair.

'I don't know how we fought. The men were trampling all over my back, and I lay low. Then our rowers on the left side—tied to their oars, you know—began to yell and back water. I could hear the water sizzle, and we spun round like a cockchafer and I knew, lying where I was, that there was a galley coming up bow-on, to ram us on the left side. I could just lift up my head and see her sail over the bulwarks. We wanted to meet her bow to bow, but it was too late. We could only turn a little bit because the galley on our right had hooked herself on to us and stopped our moving. Then, by gum! there was a crash! Our left oars began to break as the other galley, the moving one y'know, stuck her nose into them. Then the lower-deck oars shot up through the deck planking, butt first, and one of them jumped clean up into the air and came down again close to my head.'

'How was that managed?'

'The moving galley's bow was plunking them back through their own oar-holes, and I could hear the devil of a shindy in the decks below. Then her nose caught us nearly in the middle, and we tilted sideways, and the fellows in the right-hand galley unhitched their hooks and ropes, and threw things on to our upper deck—arrows, and hot pitch or something that stung, and we went up and up and up on the left side, and the right side dipped, and I twisted my head round and saw the water stand still as it topped the right bulwarks, and then it curled over and crashed down on the whole lot of us on the right side, and I felt it hit my back, and I woke.'

'One minute, Charlie. When the sea topped the bulwarks, what did it look like?' I had my reasons for asking. A man of my acquaintance had once gone down with a leaking ship in a still sea, and had seen the water-level pause for an instant ere it fell on the deck.

'It looked just like a banjo-string drawn tight, and it seemed to stay there for years,' said Charlie.

Exactly! The other man had said: 'It looked like a silver wire laid down along the bulwarks, and I thought it was never going to break.' He had paid everything except the bare life for this little valueless piece of knowledge, and I had travelled ten thousand weary miles to meet him and take his knowledge at second hand. But Charlie, the bank clerk, on twenty-five shillings a week, he who had never been out of sight of a London omnibus, knew it all. It was no consolation to me that once in his lives he had been forced to die for his gains. I also must have died scores of times, but behind me, because I could have used my knowledge, the doors were shut.

'And then?' I said, trying to put away the devil of envy.

'The funny thing was, though, in all the mess I didn't feel a bit astonished or frightened. It seemed as if I'd been in a good many fights, because I told my next man so when the row began. But that cad of an overseer on my deck wouldn't unloose our chains and give us a chance. He always said that we'd all be set free after a battle, but we never were; We never were.' Charlie shook his head mournfully.

'What a scoundrel!'

'I should say he was. He never gave us enough to eat, and sometimes we were so thirsty that we used to drink salt-water. I can taste that salt-water still.''

'Now tell me something about the harbour where the fight was fought.'

'I didn't dream about that. I know it was a harbour, though; becabse we were tied up to a ring on a white wall and all the face of the stone under water was covered with wood to prevent our ram getting chipped when the tide made us rock.'

'That's curious. Our hero commanded the galley? Didn't he?'

'Didn't he just! He stood by the bows and shouted like a good 'un. He was the man who killed the overseer.'

'But you were all drowned together, Charlie, weren't you?'

'I can't make that fit quite,' he said with a puzzled look. 'The galley must have gone down with all hands, and yet I fancy that the hero went on living afterward. Perhaps he climbed into the attacking ship. I wouldn't see that, of course. I was dead, you know.'

He shivered slightly and protested that he could remember no more.

I did not press him further, but to satisfy myself that he lay in ignorance of the workings of his own mind, deliberately introduced him to Mortimer Collins's 'Transmigration', and gave him a sketch of the plot before he opened the pages.

'What rot it all is!' he said, frankly, at the end of an hour. 'I don't understand his nonsense about the Red Planet Mars and the King, and the rest of it. Chuck me the Longfellow again.'

I handed him the book and wrote out as much as I could remember of his description of the sea-fight, appealing to him from time to time for confirmation of fact or detail. He would answer without raising his eyes from the book, as assuredly as though all his knowledge lay before him on the printed page. I spoke under the normal key of my voice that the current might not be broken, and I know that he was not aware of what he was saying, for his thoughts were out on the sea with Longfellow.

'Charlie,' I asked, 'when the rowers on the galleys mutinied how did they kill their overseers?'

'Tore up the benches and brained 'em. That happened when a heavy sea was running. An overseer on the lower deck slipped from the centre plank and fell among the rowers. They choked him to death against the side of the ship with their chained hands quite quietly, and it was too dark for the other overseer to see what had happened. When he asked, he was pulled down too and choked, and the lower deck fought their way up deck by deck, with the pieces of the broken benches banging behind 'em. How they howled!'

'And what happened after that?'

'I don't know. The hero went away—red hair and red beard

and all. That was after he had captured our galley, I think.'

The sound of my voice irritated him, and he motioned slightly with his left hand as a man does when interruption jars.

'You never told me he was red-headed before, or that he captured your galley,' I said, after a discreet interval.

Charlie did not raise his eyes.

'He was as red as a red bear,' said he, abstractedly. 'He came from the north; they said so in the galley when he looked for rowers—not slaves, but free men. Afterward—years and years afterward—news came from another ship, or else he came back—' His lips moved in silence. He was rapturously retasting some poem before him.

'Where had he been, then?' I was almost whispering that the sentence might come gentle to whichever section of Charlie's brain was working on my behalf.

'To the Beaches—the Long and Wonderful Beaches!' was the reply, after a minute of silence.

'To Furdurstrandi?' I asked, tingling from head to foot.

'Yes, to Furdurstrandi,' he pronounced the word in a new fashion 'And I too saw—' The voice failed.

'Do you know what you have said?' I shouted, incautiously.

He lifted his eyes, fully roused now. 'No!' he snapped. 'I wish you'd let a chap go on reading. Hark to this:

'But Othere, the old sea captain,
He neither paused nor stirred
Till the king listened, and then
Once more took up his pen
And wrote down every word."

'And to the King of the Saxons
In witness of the truth,
Raising his noble head,
He stretched his brown hand and said,

"Behold this walrus tooth."

'By Jove, what chaps those must have been, to go sailing all over the shop never knowing where they'd fetch the land! Hah!'

'Charlie,' I pleaded, 'if you'll only he sensible for a minute or two I'll make our hero in our tale every inch as good as Othere.'

'Umph! Longfellow wrote that poem. I don't care about writing things any more. I want to read.' He was thoroughly out of tune now, and raging over my own ill-luck, I left him.

Conceive yourself at the door of the world's treasure-house guarded by a child—an idle irresponsible child playing knuckle-bones—on whose favour depends the gift of the key, and you will imagine one-half my torment. Till that evening Charlie had spoken nothing that might not lie within the experiences of a Greek galley-slave. But now, or there was no virtue in books, he had talked of some desperate adventure of the Vikings, of Thorfin Karlsefne's sailing to Wineland, which is America, in the ninth or tenth century. The battle in the harbour he had seen; and his own death he had described. But this was a much more startling plunge into the past. Was it possible that he had skipped half a dozen lives and was then dimly remembering some episode of a thousand years later? It was a maddening jumble, and the worst of it was that Charlie Mears in his normal condition was the last person in the world to clear it up. I could only wait and watch, but I went to bed that night full of the wildest imaginings. There was nothing that was not possible if Charlie's detestable memory only held good.

I might rewrite the Saga of Thorfin Karlsefne as it had never been written before, might tell the story of the first discovery of America, myself the discoverer. But I was entirely at Charlie's mercy, and so long as there was a three-and-six-penny Bohn volume within his reach Charlie would not tell. I dared not curse him openly; I hardly dared jog his memory, for I was dealing with the experiences of a thousand years ago, told through the mouth of a boy of today; and a boy of today is affected by every change of tone and gust of opinion, so that he lies even when he desires to speak the truth.

I saw no more of him for nearly a week. When next I met him it was in Gracechurch Street with a billbook chained to his waist. Business took him over London Bridge and I accompanied him. He was very full of the importance of that book and magnified it. As we passed over the Thames we paused to look at a steamer unloading great slabs of white and brown marble. A barge drifted under the steamer's stern and a lonely cow in that barge bellowed. Charlie's face changed from the face of the bank clerk to that of an unknown and—though he would not have believed this—a much shrewder man. He flung out his arm across the parapet of the bridge, and laughing very loudly, said:

'When they heard our bulls bellow the Skroelings ran away!'

I waited only for an instant, but the barge and the cow had disappeared under the bows of the steamer before I answered.

'Charlie, what do you suppose are Skroelings?'

'Never heard of 'em before. They sound like a new kind of seagull. What a chap you are for asking questions!' he replied. 'I have to go to the cashier of the Omnibus Company yonder. Will you wait for me and we can lunch somewhere together? I've a notion for a poem.'

'No, thanks. I'm off. You're sure you know nothing about Skroelings?'

'Not unless he's been entered for the Liverpool Handicap.' He nodded and disappeared in the crowd.

Now it is written in the Saga of Eric the Red or that of Thorfin Karlsefne, that nine hundred years ago when Karlsefne's galleys came to Leif's booths, which Leif had erected in the unknown land called Markland, which may or may not have been Rhode Island, the Skroelings—and the Lord He knows who these may or may not have been—came to trade with the Vikings, and ran away because they were frightened at the bellowing of the cattle which Thorfin had brought with him in the ships. But what in the world could a Greek slave know of that affair? I wandered up and down among the streets trying to unravel the mystery, and the more I considered it, the more baffling it grew. One thing only seemed certain, and that certainty took away my breath for the moment. If I came to full knowledge of anything at all, it would not be one life of the soul in Charlie Mears's body, but half a dozen—half a dozen several and separate existences spent on blue water in the morning of the world!

Then I walked round the situation.

Obviously if I used my knowledge I should stand alone and unapproachable until all men were as wise as myself. That would be something, but manlike I was ungrateful. It seemed bitterly unfair that Charlie's memory should fail me when I needed it most. Great Powers above—I looked up at them through the fog smoke—did the Lords of Life and Death know what this meant to me? Nothing less than eternal fame of the best kind; that comes from One, and is shared by one alone. I would be content—remembering Clive, I stood astounded at my own moderation—with the mere right to tell one story, to work out one little contribution to the light literature of the day. If Charlie were permitted full recollection for one hour—for sixty short minutes—of existences that had extended over a thousand years—I would forego all profit and honour from all that I should make of his speech. I would take no share in the commotion that would follow throughout the particular corner of the earth that calls itself 'the world'. The thing should be put forth anonymously. Nay, I would make other men believe that they had written it. They would hire bull-hided self-advertising Englishmen to bellow it abroad. Preachers would found a fresh conduct of life upon it, swearing that it was new and that they had lifted the fear of death from all mankind. Every Orientalist in Europe would patronize it discursively with Sanskrit and Pali texts. Terrible women would invent unclean variants of the men's belief for the elevation of their sisters. Churches and religions would war over it. Between the hailing and re-starting of an omnibus I foresaw the scuffles that would arise among half a dozen denominations all professing 'the doctrine of the True Metempsychosis as applied to the world and the New Era'; and saw, too, the respectable English newspapers shying, like frightened kine, over the beautiful simplicity of the tale. The mind leaped forward a hundred—two hundred—a thousand years. I saw with sorrow that men would mutilate and garble the story; that rival creeds would turn it upside down till, at last, the western world which clings to the dread of death more closely than the hope of life, would set it aside as an interesting superstition and stampede after some faith so long forgotten that it seemed altogether new. Upon this I changed the terms of the bargain that I would make with the Lords of Life and Death. Only let me know, let me write, the story with sure knowledge that I wrote the truth, and I would burn the manuscript as a solemn sacrifice. Five minutes after the last line was written I would destroy it all. But I must be allowed to write it with absolute certainty.

There was no answer. The flaming colours of an Aquarium poster caught my eye and I wondered whether it would be wise or prudent to lure Charlie into the hands of the professional mesmerist, and whether, if he were under his power, he would speak of his past lives. If he did, and if people believed him...but Charlie would be frightened and flustered, or made conceited by the interviews. In either case he would begin to lie, through fear or vanity. He was safest in my own hands.

'They are very funny fools, your English,' said a voice at my elbow, and turning round I recognized a casual acquaintance, a young Bengali law student, called Grish Chunder, whose father had sent him to England to become civilized. The old man was a retired native official, and on an income of five pounds a month contrived to allow his son two hundred pounds a year, and the run of his teeth in a city where he could pretend to be the cadet of a royal house, and tell stories of the brutal Indian bureaucrats who ground the faces of the poor.

Grish Chunder was a young, fat, full-bodied Bengali dressed with scrupulous care in frock coat, tall hat, light trousers and tan gloves. But I had known him in the days when the brutal Indian Government paid for his university education, and he contributed cheap sedition to Sachi Durpan, and intrigued with the wives of his schoolmates.

'That is very funny and very foolish,' he said, nodding at the poster. 'I am going down to the Northbrook Club. Will you come too?'

I walked with him for some time. 'You are not well,' he said. 'What is there in your mind? You do not talk.'

'Grish Chunder, you've been too well educated to believe in a God, haven't you?'

'Oah, yes, here! But when I go home I must conciliate popular superstition, and make ceremonies of purification, and my women will anoint idols.'

'And hang up tulsi and feast the purohit, and take you back into caste again and make a good khuttri of you again, you advanced social Free-thinker. And you'll eat desi food, and like it all, from the smell in the courtyard to the mustard oil over you.'

'I shall very much like it,' said Grish Chunder, unguardedly. 'Once a Hindu—always a Hindu. But I like to know what the English think they know.'

'I'll tell you something that one Englishman knows. It's an old tale to you.'

I began to tell the story of Charlie in English, but Grish Chunder put a question in the vernacular, and the history went forward naturally in the tongue best suited for its telling. After all it could never have been told in English. Grish Chunder heard me, nodding from time to time, and then came up to my rooms where I finished the tale.

'Beshak,' he said, philosophically. 'Lekin darwaza band hai. (Without doubt, but the door is shut.) I have heard of this remembering of previous existences among my people. It is of course an old tale with us, but, to happen to an Englishman—a cow-fed Malechk—an outcast. By Jove, that is most peculiar!'

'Outcast yourself, Grish Chunder! You eat cow-beef every day. Let's think the thing over. The boy remembers his incarnations.'

'Does he know that?' said Grish Chunder, quietly, swinging his legs as he sat on my table. He was speaking in English now.

'He does not know anything. Would I speak to you if he did? Go on!'

'There is no going on at all. If you tell that to your friends they will say you are mad and put it in the papers. Suppose, now, you prosecute for libel.'

'Let's leave that out of the question entirely. Is there any chance of his being made to speak?'

'There is a chance. Oah, yess! But if he spoke it would mean that all this world would end now—instanto—fall down on your head. These things are not allowed, you know. As I said, the door is shut.'

'Not a ghost of a chance?'

'How can there be? You are a Christian, and it is forbidden to eat, in your books, of the Tree of Life, or else you would never die. How shall you all fear death if you all know what your friend does not know that he knows? I am afraid to be kicked, but I am not afraid to die, because I know what I know. You are not afraid to be kicked, but you are afraid to die. If you were not, by God! you English would be all over the shop in an hour, upsetting the balances of power, and making commotions. It would not be good. But no fear. He will remember a little and a little less, and he will call it dreams. Then he will forget altogether. When I passed my First Arts Examination in Calcutta that was all in the crambook on Wordsworth. Trailing clouds of glory, you know.'

'This seems to be an exception to the rule.'

'There are no exceptions to rules. Some are not so hard-looking as others, but they are all the same when you touch. If this friend of yours said so-and-so and so-and-so, indicating that he remembered all his lost lives, or one piece of a lost life, he would not be in the bank another hour. He would be what you called sack because he was mad, and they would send him to an asylum for lunatics. You can see that, my friend.'

'Of course I can, but I wasn't thinking of him. His name need never appear in the story.'

'Ah! I see. That story will never be written. You can try.'

'I am going to.'

'For your own credit and for the sake of money, of course?'

'No. For the sake of writing the story. On my honour that will be all.'

'Even then there is no chance. You cannot play with the Gods. It is a very pretty story now. As they say, Let it go on that—I mean at that. Be quick; he will not last long.'

'How do you mean?'

'What I say. He has never, so far, thought about a woman.'

'Hasn't he though!' I remembered some of Charlie's confidences.

'I mean no woman has thought about him. When that comes; bus—hogya—all up' I know. There are millions of women here. Housemaids, for instance.'

I winced at the thought of my story being ruined by a housemaid. And yet nothing was more probable.

Grish Chunder grinned.

'Yes-also pretty girls-cousins of his house, and perhaps not of his house. One kiss that he gives back again and remembers will cure all this nonsense. or else—'

'Or else what? Remember he does not know that he knows.'

'I know that. Or else, if nothing happens he will become immersed in the trade and the financial speculations like the rest. It must be so. You can see that it must be so. But the woman will come first, I think.'

There was a rap at the door, and Charlie charged in impetuously. He had been released from office, and by the look in his eyes I could see that he had come over for a long talk; most probably with poems in his pockets. Charlie's poems were very wearying, but sometimes they led him to talk about the galley.

Grish Chunder looked at him keenly for a minute.

'I beg your pardon,' Charlie said, uneasily; 'I didn't know you had any one with you.'

'I am going,' said Grish Chunder.

He drew me into the lobby as he departed.

'That is your man,' he said, quickly. 'I tell you he will never speak all you wish. That is rot—bosh. But he would be most good to make to see things. Suppose now we pretend that it was only play'—I had never seen Grish Chunder so excited 'and pour the ink-pool into his hand. Eh, what do you think? I tell you that he could see anything that a man could see. Let me get the ink and the camphor. He is a seer and he will tell us very many things.'

'He may be all you say, but I'm not going to trust him to your gods and devils.'

'It will not hurt him. He will only feel a little stupid and dull when he wakes up. You have seen boys look into the ink-pool before.'

'That is the reason why I am not going to see it any more. You'd better go, Grish Chunder.'

He went, declaring far down the staircase that it was throwing away my only chance of looking into the future.

This left me unmoved, for I was concerned for the past, and no peering of hypnotized boys into mirrors and ink-pools would help me do that. But I recognized Grish Chunder's point of view and sympathized with it.

'What a big black brute that was!' said Charlie, when I returned to him. 'Well, look here, I've just done a poem; did it instead of playing dominoes after lunch. May I read it?'

'Let me read it to myself.'

'Then you miss the proper expression. Besides, you always make my things sound as if the rhymes were all wrong.'

'Read it aloud, then. You're like the rest of 'em.'

Charlie mouthed me his poem, and it was not much worse than the average of his verses. He had been reading his book faithfully, but he was not pleased when I told him that I preferred my Longfellow undiluted with Charlie.

Then we began to go through the MS. line by line; Charlie parrying every objection and correction with:

'Yes, that may be better, but you don't catch what I'm driving at.'

Charlie was, in one way at least, very like one kind of poet.

There was a pencil scrawl at the back of the paper and 'What's that?' I said.

'Oh that's not poetry at all. It's some rot I wrote last night before I went to bed and it was too much bother to hunt for rhymes; so I made it a sort of a blank verse instead.'

Here is Charlie's 'blank verse':

'We pulled for you when the wind was against us and the sails were low.

Will you never let us go?

We ate bread and onions when you took towns or ran aboard quickly when you were beaten back by the foe.

The captains walked up and down the deck in fair weather singing songs, but we were below.

We fainted with our chins on the oars and you did

not see that we were idle for we still swung to and fro.

Will you never let us go?

The salt made the oar handles like sharkskin; our knees were cut to the bone with salt cracks; our hair was stuck to our foreheads; and our lips were cut to our gums and you whipped us because we could not row.

Will you never let us go?

But in a little time we shall run out of the portholes as the water runs along the oarblade, and though you tell the others to row after us you will never catch us till you catch the oar-thresh and tie up the winds in the belly of the sail. Aho!

Will you never let us go?'

'H'm. What's oar-thresh, Charlie?'

'The water washed up by the oars. That's the sort of song they might sing in the galley, y'know. Aren't you ever going to finish that story and give me some of the profits?'

'It depends on yourself. If you had only told me more about your hero in the first instance it might have been finished by now. You're so hazy in your notions.'

'I only want to give you the general notion of it—the knocking about from place to place and the fighting and all

6

MY SON'S WIFE

THE FLOODS

The rain it rains without a stay
In the hills above us, in the hills;
And presently the floods break way
Whose strength is in the hills.
The trees they suck from every cloud,
The valley brooks they roar aloud—
Bank-high for the lowlands, lowlands,
Lowlands under the hills!

The first wood down is sere and small,
From the hills, the brishings off the hills;
And then come by the bats and all
We cut last year in the hills;
And then the roots we tried to cleave
But found too tough and had to leave—
Polting through the lowlands, lowlands,
Lowlands under the hills!

The eye shall look, the ear shall hark
To the hills, the doings in the hills,

And rivers mating in the dark
With tokens from the hills.
Now what is weak will surely go,
And what is strong must prove it so.
Stand fast in the lowlands, lowlands,
Lowlands under the hills!

The floods they shall not be afraid—
Nor the hills above 'em, nor the hills—
Of any fence which man has made
Betwixt him and the hills.
The waters shall not reckon twice
For any work of man's device,
But bid it down to the lowlands, lowlands,
Lowlands under the hills!

The floods shall sweep corruption clean—
By the hills, the blessing of the hills—
That more the meadows may be green
New-amended from the hills.
The crops and cattle shall increase,
Nor little children shall not cease—
Go—plough the lowlands, lowlands,
Lowlands under the hills!

THE FABULISTS

When all the world would have a matter hid,
Since Truth is seldom friend to any crowd,
Men write in fable, as old Æsop did,
Jesting at that which none will name aloud.
And this they needs must do, or it will fall
Unless they please they are not heard at all.

When desperate Folly daily laboureth
To work confusion upon all we have,
When diligent Sloth demandeth Freedom's death,
And banded Fear commandeth Honour's grave--
Even in that certain hour before the fall
Unless men please they are not heard at all.

Needs must all please, yet some not all for need
Needs must all toil, yet some not all for gain,
But that men taking pleasure may take heed,
Whom present toil shall snatch from later pain.
Thus some have toiled but their reward was small
Since, though they pleased, they were not heard at all.

This was the lock that lay upon our lips,
This was the yoke that we have undergone,
Denying us all pleasant fellowships
As in our time and generation.
Our pleasures unpursued age past recall.
And for our pains--we are not heard at all.

What man hears aught except the groaning guns?
What man heeds aught save what each instant brings?
When each man's life all imaged life outruns,
What man shall pleasure in imaginings?
So it hath fallen, as it was bound to fall,
We are not, nor we were not, heard at all.

He had suffered from the disease of the century since his early youth, and before he was thirty he was heavily marked with it. He and a few friends had rearranged Heaven very comfortably, but the re-organization of Earth, which they called Society, was even greater fun. It demanded Work in the shape of many taxi-rides daily; hours of brilliant talk with brilliant talkers; some sparkling correspondence; a few silences (but on the understanding that their own turn should come soon) while other people expounded philosophies; and a fair number of picture-galleries, tea-fights, concerts, theatres, music-halls, and cinema shows; the whole trimmed with love-making to women whose hair smelt of cigarette-smoke. Such strong days sent Frankwell Midmore back to his flat assured that he and his friends had helped the World a step nearer the Truth, the Dawn, and the New Order.

His temperament, he said, led him more towards concrete data than abstract ideas. People who investigate detail are apt to be tired at the day's end. The same temperament, or it may have been a woman, made him early attach himself to the Immoderate Left of his Cause in the capacity of an experimenter in Social Relations. And since the Immoderate Left contains plenty of women anxious to help earnest inquirers with large independent incomes to arrive at evaluations of essentials, Frankwell Midmore's lot was far from contemptible.

At that hour Fate chose to play with him. A widowed aunt, widely separated by nature, and more widely by marriage, from all that Midmore's mother had ever been or desired to be, died and left him possessions. Mrs Midmore, having that summer embraced a creed which denied the existence of death, naturally could not stoop to burial; but Midmore had to leave London for the dank country at a season when Social Regeneration works best through long, cushioned conferences, two by two, after tea. There he faced the bracing ritual of the British funeral, and was wept at across the raw grave by an elderly coffin-shaped female with a long nose, who called him 'Master Frankie'; and there he was congratulated behind an echoing top-hat by a man he mistook for a mute, who turned out to be his aunt's lawyer. He wrote his mother next day, after a bright account of the funeral:

'So far as I can understand, she has left me between four and five hundred a year. It all comes from Ther Land, as they call it down here. The unspeakable attorney, Sperrit, and a green-eyed daughter, who hums to herself as she tramps but is silent on all subjects except 'huntin', insisted on taking me to see it. Ther Land is brown and green in alternate slabs like chocolate and pistachio cakes, speckled with occasional peasants who do not utter. In case it should not be wet enough there is a wet brook in the middle of it. Ther House is by the brook. I shall look into it later. If there should be any little memento of Jenny that you care for, let me know. Didn't you tell me that mid-Victorian furniture is coming into the market again? Jenny's old maid—it is called Rhoda Dolbie—tells me that Jenny promised it thirty pounds a year. The will does not. Hence, I suppose, the tears at the funeral. But that is close on ten per cent of the income. I fancy Jenny has destroyed all her private papers and records of her vie intime, if, indeed, life be possible in such a place. The Sperrit man told me that if I had means of my own I might come and live on Ther Land. I didn't tell him how much I would pay not to! I cannot think it right that any human being should exercise mastery over others in the merciless fashion our tom-fool social system permits; so, as it is all mine, I intend to sell it whenever the unholy Sperrit can find a purchaser.'

And he went to Mr Sperrit with the idea next day, just before returning to town.

'Quite so,' said the lawyer. 'I see your point, of course. But the house itself is rather old-fashioned—hardly the type purchasers demand nowadays. There's no park, of course, and the bulk of the land is let to a life-tenant, a Mr Sidney. As long as he pays his rent, he can't be turned out, and even if he didn't'—Mr Sperrit's face relaxed a shade—'you might have a difficulty.'

'The property brings four hundred a year, I understand,' said Midmore.

'Well, hardly—ha-ardly. Deducting land and income tax, tithes, fire insurance, cost of collection and repairs of course, it returned two hundred and eighty-four pounds last year. The repairs are rather a large item—owing to the brook. I call it Liris—out of Horace, you know.'

Midmore looked at his watch impatiently.

'I suppose you can find somebody to buy it?' he repeated.

'We will do our best, of course, if those are your instructions. Then, that is all except'—here Midmore half rose, but Mr Sperrit's little grey eyes held his large brown ones firmly—'except about Rhoda Dolbie, Mrs Werf's maid. I may tell you that we did not draw up your aunt's last will. She grew secretive towards the last—elderly people often do—and had it done in London. I expect her memory failed her, or she mislaid her notes. She used to put them in her spectacle-case... My motor only takes eight minutes to get to the station, Mr Midmore...but, as I was saying, whenever she made her will with us, Mrs Werf always left Rhoda thirty pounds per annum. Charlie, the wills!' A clerk with a baldish head and a long nose dealt documents on to the table like cards, and breathed heavily behind Midmore. 'It's in no sense a legal obligation, of course,' said Mr Sperrit. 'Ah, that one is dated January the 11th, 1889.'

Midmore looked at his watch again and found himself saying with no good grace: 'Well, I suppose she'd better have it—for the present at any rate.'

He escaped with an uneasy feeling that two hundred and fifty-four pounds a year was not exactly four hundred, and that Charlie's long nose annoyed him. Then he returned, first-class, to his own affairs.

Of the two, perhaps three, experiments in Social Relations which he had then in hand, one interested him acutely. It had run for some months and promised most variegated and interesting developments, on which he dwelt luxuriously all the way to town. When he reached his flat he was not well prepared for a twelve-page letter explaining, in the diction of the Immoderate

Left which rubricates its I's and illuminates its T's, that the lady had realized greater attractions in another Soul. She re-stated, rather than pleaded, the gospel of the Immoderate Left as her justification, and ended in an impassioned demand for her right to express herself in and on her own life, through which, she pointed out, she could pass but once. She added that if, later, she should discover Midmore was 'essentially complementary to her needs,' she would tell him so. That Midmore had himself written much the same sort of epistle—barring the hint of return—to a woman of whom his needs for self-expression had caused him to weary three years before, did not assist him in the least. He expressed himself to the gas fire in terms essential but not complimentary. Then he reflected on the detached criticism of his best friends and her best friends, male and female, with whom he and she and others had talked so openly while their gay adventure was in flower. He recalled, too—this must have been about midnight—her analysis from every angle, remote and most intimate, of the mate to whom she had been adjudged under the base convention which is styled marriage. Later, at that bad hour when the cattle wake for a little, he remembered her in other aspects and went down into the hell appointed; desolate, desiring, with no God to call upon. About eleven o'clock next morning Eliphaz the Temanite, Bildad the Shuhite, and Zophar the Naamathite called upon him 'for they had made appointment together' to see how he took it; but the janitor told them that Job had gone—into the country, he believed.

Midmore's relief when he found his story was not written across his aching temples for Mr Sperrit to read—the defeated lover, like the successful one, believes all earth privy to his soul—was put down by Mr Sperrit to quite different causes. He led him into a morning-room. The rest of the house seemed to be full of people, singing to a loud piano idiotic songs about cows, and the hall smelt of damp cloaks.

'It's our evening to take the winter cantata,' Mr Sperrit

explained. 'It's "High Tide on the Coast of Lincolnshire". I hoped you'd come back. There are scores of little things to settle. As for the house, of course, it stands ready for you at any time. I couldn't get Rhoda out of it—nor could Charlie for that matter. She's the sister, isn't she, of the nurse who brought you down here when you were four, she says, to recover from measles?'

'Is she? Was I?' said Midmore through the bad tastes in his mouth. 'D'you suppose I could stay there the night?'

Thirty joyous young voices shouted appeal to some one to leave their 'pipes of parsley 'ollow—'ollow—'ollow!' Mr Sperrit had to raise his voice above the din.

'Well, if I asked you to stay here, I should never hear the last of it from Rhoda. She's a little cracked, of course, but the soul of devotion and capable of anything. Ne sit ancillae, you know.'

'Thank you. Then I'll go. I'll walk.' He stumbled out dazed and sick into the winter twilight, and sought the square house by the brook.

It was not a dignified entry, because when the door was unchained and Rhoda exclaimed, he took two valiant steps into the hall and then fainted—as men sometimes will after twenty-two hours of strong emotion and little food.

'I'm sorry,' he said when he could speak. He was lying at the foot of the stairs, his head on Rhoda's lap.

'Your 'ome is your castle, sir,' was the reply in his hair. 'I smelt it wasn't drink. You lay on the sofa till I get your supper.'

She settled him in a drawing-room hung with yellow silk, heavy with the smell of dead leaves and oil lamp. Something murmured soothingly in the background and overcame the noises in his head. He thought he heard horses' feet on wet gravel and a voice singing about ships and flocks and grass. It passed close to the shuttered bay-window.

'But each will mourn his own, she saith,
And sweeter woman ne'er drew breath

Than my son's wife, Elizabeth...
Cusha—cusha—cusha—calling.'

The hoofs broke into a canter as Rhoda entered with the tray. 'And then I'll put you to bed,' she said. 'Sidney's coming in the morning.' Midmore asked no questions. He dragged his poor bruised soul to bed and would have pitied it all over again, but the food and warm sherry and water drugged him to instant sleep.

Rhoda's voice wakened him, asking whether he would have ''ip, foot, or sitz', which he understood were the baths of the establishment. 'Suppose you try all three,' she suggested. 'They're all yours, you know, sir.'

He would have renewed his sorrows with the daylight, but her words struck him pleasantly. Everything his eyes opened upon was his very own to keep for ever. The carved four-post Chippendale bed, obviously worth hundreds; the wavy walnut William and Mary chairs—he had seen worse ones labelled twenty guineas apiece; the oval medallion mirror; the delicate eighteenth-century wire fireguard; the heavy brocaded curtains were his—all his. So, too, a great garden full of birds that faced him when he shaved; a mulberry tree, a sun-dial, and a dull, steel-coloured brook that murmured level with the edge of a lawn a hundred yards away. Peculiarly and privately his own was the smell of sausages and coffee that he sniffed at the head of the wide square landing, all set round with mysterious doors and Bartolozzi prints. He spent two hours after breakfast in exploring his new possessions. His heart leaped up at such things as sewing-machines, a rubber-tyred bath-chair in a tiled passage, a malachite-headed Malacca cane, boxes and boxes of unopened stationery, seal-rings, bunches of keys, and at the bottom of a steel-net reticule a little leather purse with seven pounds ten shillings in gold and eleven shillings in silver.

'You used to play with that when my sister brought you down here after your measles,' said Rhoda as he slipped the money into his pocket. 'Now, this was your pore dear auntie's business-room.'

She opened a low door. 'Oh, I forgot about Mr Sidney! There he is.' An enormous old man with rheumy red eyes that blinked under downy white eyebrows sat in an Empire chair, his cap in his hands. Rhoda withdrew sniffing. The man looked Midmore over in silence, then jerked a thumb towards the door. 'I reckon she told you who I be,' he began. 'I'm the only farmer you've got. Nothin' goes off my place 'thout it walks on its own feet. What about my pig-pound?'

'Well, what about it?' said Midmore.

'That's just what I be come about. The County Councils are getting more particular. Did ye know there was swine fever at Pashell's? There be. It'll 'ave to be in brick.'

'Yes,' said Midmore politely.

'I've bin at your aunt that was, plenty times about it. I don't say she wasn't a just woman, but she didn't read the lease same way I did. I be used to bein' put upon, but there's no doing any longer 'thout that pig-pound.'

'When would you like it?' Midmore asked. It seemed the easiest road to take.

'Any time or other suits me, I reckon. He ain't thrivin' where he is, an' I paid eighteen shillin' for him.' He crossed his hands on his stick and gave no further sign of life.

'Is that all?' Midmore stammered.

'All now—excep'—he glanced fretfully at the table beside him—'excep' my usuals. Where's that Rhoda?'

Midmore rang the bell. Rhoda came in with a bottle and a glass. The old man helped himself to four stiff fingers, rose in one piece, and stumped out. At the door he cried ferociously: 'Don't suppose it's any odds to you whether I'm drowned or not, but them floodgates want a wheel and winch, they do. I be too old for liftin' 'em with the bar—my time o' life.'

'Good riddance if 'e was drowned,' said Rhoda. 'But don't you mind him. He's only amusin' himself. Your pore dear auntie used to give 'im 'is usual—'tisn't the whisky you drink—an' send 'im about 'is business.'

'I see. Now, is a pig-pound the same thing as a pig-sty?'

Rhoda nodded. ''E needs one, too, but 'e ain't entitled to it. You look at 'is lease—third drawer on the left in that Bombay cab'net—an' next time 'e comes you ask 'im to read it. That'll choke 'im off, because 'e can't!'

There was nothing in Midmore's past to teach him the message and significance of a hand-written lease of the late 'eighties, but Rhoda interpreted.

'It don't mean anything reelly,' was her cheerful conclusion, 'excep' you mustn't get rid of him anyhow, an' 'e can do what 'e likes always. Lucky for us 'e do farm; and if it wasn't for 'is woman—'

'Oh, there's a Mrs Sidney, is there?'

'Lor, no!' The Sidneys don't marry. They keep. That's his fourth since—to my knowledge. He was a takin' man from the first.'

'Any families?'

'They'd be grown up by now if there was, wouldn't they? But you can't spend all your days considerin' 'is interests. That's what gave your pore aunt 'er indigestion. 'Ave you seen the gun-room?'

Midmore held strong views on the immorality of taking life for pleasure. But there was no denying that the late Colonel Werf's seventy-guinea breechloaders were good at their filthy job. He loaded one, took it out and pointed—merely pointed—it at a cock-pheasant which rose out of a shrubbery behind the kitchen, and the flaming bird came down in a long slant on the lawn, stone dead. Rhoda from the scullery said it was a lovely shot, and told him lunch was ready.

He spent the afternoon gun in one hand, a map in the other, beating the bounds of his lands. They lay altogether in a shallow, uninteresting valley, flanked with woods and bisected by a brook. Up stream was his own house; down stream, less than half a mile, a low red farm-house squatted in an old orchard, beside what looked like small lock-gates on the Thames. There was no doubt as to ownership. Mr Sidney saw him while yet far off, and bellowed at him about pig-pounds and floodgates. These last were two great sliding shutters of weedy oak across the brook, which were prised up inch by inch with a crowbar along a notched strip of iron, and when Sidney opened them they at once let out half the water. Midmore watched it shrink between its aldered banks like some conjuring trick. This, too, was his very own.

'I see,' he said. 'How interesting! Now, what's that bell for?' he went on, pointing to an old ship's bell in a rude belfry at the end of an outhouse. 'Was that a chapel once?' The red-eyed giant seemed to have difficulty in expressing himself for the moment and blinked savagely.

'Yes,' he said at last. 'My chapel. When you 'ear that bell ring you'll 'ear something. Nobody but me 'ud put up with it—but I reckon it don't make any odds to you.' He slammed the gates down again, and the brook rose behind them with a suck and a grunt.

Midmore moved off, conscious that he might be safer with Rhoda to hold his conversational hand. As he passed the front of the farm-house a smooth fat woman, with neatly parted grey hair under a widow's cap, curtsied to him deferentially through the window. By every teaching of the Immoderate Left she had a perfect right to express herself in any way she pleased, but the curtsey revolted him. And on his way home he was hailed from behind a hedge by a manifest idiot with no roof to his mouth, who hallooed and danced round him.

'What did that beast want?' he demanded of Rhoda at tea.

'Jimmy? He only wanted to know if you 'ad any telegrams to send. 'E'll go anywhere so long as 'tisn't across running water. That gives 'im 'is seizures. Even talkin' about it for fun like makes 'im shake.'

'But why isn't he where he can be properly looked after?'

'What 'arm's 'e doing? 'E's a love-child, but 'is family can pay for 'im. If 'e was locked up 'e'd die all off at once, like a wild rabbit. Won't you, please, look at the drive, sir?'

Midmore looked in the fading light. The neat gravel was pitted with large roundish holes, and there was a punch or two of the same sort on the lawn.

'That's the 'unt comin' 'ome,' Rhoda explained. 'Your pore dear auntie always let 'em use our drive for a short cut after the Colonel died. The Colonel wouldn't so much because he preserved; but your auntie was always an 'orsewoman till 'er sciatica.'

'Isn't there some one who can rake it over or—or something?' said Midmore vaguely.

'Oh yes. You'll never see it in the morning, but—you was out when they came 'ome an' Mister Fisher—he's the Master—told me to tell you with 'is compliments that if you wasn't preservin' and cared to 'old to the old understanding, 'is gravel-pit is at your service same as before. 'E thought, perhaps, you mightn't know, and it 'ad slipped my mind to tell you. It's good gravel, Mister Fisher's, and it binds beautiful on the drive. We 'ave to draw it, o' course, from the pit, but—'

Midmore looked at her helplessly.

'Rhoda,' said he, 'what am I supposed to do?'

'Oh, let 'em come through,' she replied. 'You never know. You may want to 'unt yourself some day.'

That evening it rained and his misery returned on him, the worse for having been diverted. At last he was driven to paw over a few score books in a panelled room called the library, and realized with horror what the late Colonel Werf's mind must have been in its prime. The volumes smelt of a dead world as strongly as they did of mildew. He opened and thrust them back, one after another, till crude coloured illustrations of men on horses held his eye. He began at random and read a little, moved into the drawing-room with the volume, and settled down by the fire still reading. It was a foul world into which he peeped for the first time—a heavy-eating, hard-drinking hell of horse-copers, swindlers, matchmaking mothers, economically dependent virgins selling themselves blushingly for cash and lands; Jews, tradesmen, and an ill-considered spawn of Dickens-and-horsedung characters (I give Midmore's own criticism), but he read on, fascinated, and behold, from the pages leaped, as it were, the brother to the red-eyed man of the brook, bellowing at a landlord (here Midmore realized that he was that very animal) for new barns; and another man who, like himself again, objected to hoof-marks on gravel. Outrageous as thought and conception were, the stuff seemed to have the rudiments of observation. He dug out other volumes by the same author, till Rhoda came in with a silver candlestick.

'Rhoda,' said he, 'did you ever hear about a character called James Pigg—and Batsey?'

'Why, o' course,' said she. 'The Colonel used to come into the kitchen in 'is dressin'-gown an' read us all those Jorrockses.'

'Oh, Lord!' said Midmore, and went to bed with a book called 'Handley Cross' under his arm, and a lonelier Columbus into a stranger world the wet-ringed moon never looked upon.

Here we omit much. But Midmore never denied that for the epicure in sensation the urgent needs of an ancient house, as interpreted by Rhoda pointing to daylight through attic-tiles held in place by moss, gives an edge to the pleasure of Social Research elsewhere. Equally he found that the reaction following prolonged research loses much of its grey terror if one knows one can at will bathe the soul in the society of plumbers (all the water-pipes had chronic appendicitis), village idiots (Jimmy had taken Midmore under his weak wing and camped daily at the drive-gates), and a giant with red eyelids whose every action is an unpredictable outrage.

Towards spring Midmore filled his house with a few friends of the Immoderate Left. It happened to be the day when, all things and Rhoda working together, a cartload of bricks, another of sand, and some bags of lime had been despatched to build Sidney his almost daily-demanded pig-pound. Midmore took his friends across the flat fields with some idea of showing them Sidney as a type of 'the peasantry'. They hit the minute when Sidney, hoarse with rage, was ordering bricklayer, mate, carts and all off his premises. The visitors disposed themselves to listen.

'You never give me no notice about changin' the pig,' Sidney shouted. The pig—at least eighteen inches long—reared on end in the old sty and smiled at the company.

'But, my good man—' Midmore opened.

'I ain't! For aught you know I be a dam' sight worse than you be. You can't come and be'ave arbit'ry with me. You are be'avin' arbit'ry! All you men go clean away an' don't set foot on my land till I bid ye.'

'But you asked'—Midmore felt his voice jump up—'to have the pig-pound built.'

"Spose I did. That's no reason you shouldn't send me notice to change the pig. 'Comin' down on me like this 'thout warnin'! That pig's got to be got into the cowshed an' all.'

'Then open the door and let him run in,' said Midmore.

'Don't you be'ave arbit'ry with me ! Take all your dam' men 'ome off my land. I won't be treated arbit'ry.'

The carts moved off without a word, and Sidney went into the house and slammed the door.

'Now, I hold that is enormously significant,' said a visitor. 'Here you have the logical outcome of centuries of feudal oppression—the frenzy of fear.' The company looked at Midmore with grave pain.

'But he did worry my life out about his pig-sty,' was all Midmore found to say.

Others took up the parable and proved to him if he only held true to the gospels of the Immoderate Left the earth would soon be covered with 'jolly little' pig-sties, built in the intervals of morris-dancing by 'the peasant' himself.

Midmore felt grateful when the door opened again and Mr Sidney invited them all to retire to the road which, he pointed out, was public. As they turned the corner of the house, a smooth-faced woman in a widow's cap curtsied to each of them through the window.

Instantly they drew pictures of that woman's lot, deprived of all vehicle for self-expression—'the set grey life and apathetic end,' one quoted—and they discussed the tremendous significance of village theatricals. Even a month ago Midmore would have told them all that he knew and Rhoda had dropped about Sidney's forms of self-expression. Now, for some strange reason, he was content to let the talk run on from village to metropolitan and world drama.

Rhoda advised him after the visitors left that 'if he wanted to do that again' he had better go up to town.

'But we only sat on cushions on the floor,' said her master.

'They're too old for romps,' she retorted, 'an' it's only the beginning of things. I've seen what I've seen. Besides, they talked and laughed in the passage going to their baths—such as took 'em.'

'Don't be a fool, Rhoda,' said Midmore. No man—unless he has loved her—will casually dismiss a woman on whose lap he has laid his head.

'Very good,' she snorted, 'but that cuts both ways. An' now, you go down to Sidney's this evenin' and put him where he ought to be. He was in his right about you givin' 'im notice about changin' the pig, but he 'adn't any right to turn it up before your company. No manners, no pig-pound. He'll understand.'

Midmore did his best to make him. He found himself reviling the old man in speech and with a joy quite new in all his experience. He wound up—it was a plagiarism from a plumber—by telling Mr Sidney that he looked like a turkey-cock, had the morals of a parish bull, and need never hope for a new pig-pound as long as he or Midmore lived.

'Very good,' said the giant. 'I reckon you thought you 'ad something against me, and now you've come down an' told it me like man to man. Quite right. I don't bear malice. Now, you send along those bricks an' sand, an' I'll make a do to build the pig-pound myself. If you look at my lease you'll find out you're bound to provide me materials for the repairs. Only—only I thought there'd be no 'arm in my askin' you to do it throughout like.'

Midmore fairly gasped. 'Then, why the devil did you turn my carts back when—when I sent them up here to do it throughout for you?'

Mr Sidney sat down on the floodgates, his eyebrows knitted in thought.

'I'll tell you,' he said slowly. '"Twas too dam' like cheatin' a suckin' baby. My woman, she said so too.'

For a few seconds the teachings of the Immoderate Left, whose humour is all their own, wrestled with those of Mother Earth, who has her own humours. Then Midmore laughed till he could scarcely stand. In due time Mr Sidney laughed too—crowing and wheezing crescendo till it broke from him in roars. They shook hands, and Midmore went home grateful that he had held his tongue among his companions.

When he reached his house he met three or four men and women on horse-back, very muddy indeed, coming down the drive. Feeling hungry himself, he asked them if they were hungry. They said they were, and he bade them enter. Jimmy took their horses, who seemed to know him. Rhoda took their battered hats, led the women upstairs for hairpins, and presently fed them all with tea-cakes, poached eggs, anchovy toast, and drinks from a coromandel-wood liqueur case which Midmore had never known that he possessed.

'And I will say,' said Miss Connie Sperrit, her spurred foot on the fender and a smoking muffin in her whip hand, 'Rhoda does one top-hole. She always did since I was eight.'

'Seven, Miss, was when you began to 'unt,' said Rhoda, setting down more buttered toast.

'And so,' the M.F.H. was saying to Midmore, 'when he got to your brute Sidney's land, we had to whip 'em off. It's a regular Alsatia for 'em. They know it. Why'—he dropped his voice—'I don't want to say anything against Sidney as your tenant, of course, but I do believe the old scoundrel's perfectly capable of putting down poison.'

'Sidney's capable of anything,' said Midmore with immense feeling; but once again he held his tongue. They were a queer community; yet when they had stamped and jingled out to their horses again, the house felt hugely big and disconcerting.

This may be reckoned the conscious beginning of his double life. It ran in odd channels that summer—a riding school, for instance, near Hayes Common and a shooting ground near Wormwood Scrubs. A man who has been saddle-galled or shoulder-bruised for half the day is not at his London best of evenings; and when the bills for his amusements come in he curtails his expenses in other directions. So a cloud settled on Midmore's name. His London world talked of a hardening of heart and a tightening of purse-strings which signified disloyalty to the Cause. One man, a confidant of the old expressive days, attacked him robustiously and demanded account of his soul's progress. It was not furnished, for Midmore was calculating how much it would cost to repave stables so dilapidated that even the village idiot apologized for putting visitors' horses into them. The man went away, and served up what he had heard of the pig-pound episode as a little newspaper sketch, calculated to annoy. Midmore read it with an eye as practical as a woman's, and since most of his experiences had been among women, at once sought out a woman to whom he might tell his sorrow at the disloyalty of his own familiar friend.

She was so sympathetic that he went on to confide how his bruised heart—she knew all about it—had found solace, with a long O, in another quarter which he indicated rather carefully in case it might be betrayed to other loyal friends. As his hints pointed directly towards facile Hampstead, and as his urgent business was the purchase of a horse from a dealer, Beckenham way, he felt he had done good work. Later, when his friend, the scribe, talked to him alluringly of 'secret gardens' and those solaces to which every man who follows the Wider Morality is entitled, Midmore lent him a five-pound note which he had got back on the price of a ninety-guinea bay gelding. So true it is, as he read in one of the late Colonel Werf's books, that 'the young man of the present day would sooner lie under an imputation against his morals than against his knowledge of horse-flesh'.

Midmore desired more than he desired anything else at that moment to ride and, above all, to jump on a ninety-guinea bay gelding with black points and a slovenly habit of hitting his fences. He did not wish many people except Mr Sidney, who very kindly lent his soft meadow behind the floodgates, to be privy to the matter, which he rightly foresaw would take him to the autumn. So he told such friends as hinted at country week-end visits that he had practically let his newly inherited house. The rent, he said, was an object to him, for he had lately lost large sums through ill-considered benevolences. He would name no names, but they could guess. And they guessed loyally all round the circle of his acquaintance as they spread the news that explained so much.

There remained only one couple of his once intimate associates to pacify. They were deeply sympathetic and utterly loyal, of course, but as curious as any of the apes whose diet they had adopted. Midmore met them in a suburban train, coming up to town, not twenty minutes after he had come off two hours' advanced tuition (one guinea an hour) over hurdles in a hall. He had, of course, changed his kit, but his too heavy bridle-hand shook a little among the newspapers. On the inspiration of the moment, which is your natural liar's best hold, he told them that he was condemned to a rest-cure. He would lie in semi-darkness drinking milk, for weeks and weeks, cut off even from letters. He was astonished and delighted at the ease with which the usual lie confounds the unusual intellect. They swallowed it as swiftly as they recommended him to live on nuts and fruit; but he saw in the woman's eyes the exact reason she would set forth for his retirement. After all, she had as much right to express herself as he purposed to take for himself; and Midmore believed strongly in the fullest equality of the sexes.

That retirement made one small ripple in the strenuous world. The lady who had written the twelve-page letter ten months before sent him another of eight pages, analysing all the motives that were leading her back to him—should she come?—now that he was ill and alone. Much might yet be retrieved, she said, out of the waste of jarring lives and piteous misunderstandings. It needed only a hand.

But Midmore needed two, next morning very early, for a devil's diversion, among wet coppices, called 'cubbing'.

'You haven't a bad seat,' said Miss Sperrit through the morning-mists. 'But you're worrying him.'

'He pulls so,' Midmore grunted.

'Let him alone, then. Look out for the branches,' she shouted, as they whirled up a splashy ride. Cubs were plentiful. Most of the hounds attached themselves to a straight-necked youngster of education who scuttled out of the woods into the open fields below.

'Hold on!' some one shouted. 'Turn 'em, Midmore. That's your brute Sidney's land. It's all wire.'

'Oh, Connie, stop!' Mrs Sperrit shrieked as her daughter charged at a boundary-hedge.

'Wire be damned! I had it all out a fortnight ago. Come on!' This was Midmore, buffeting into it a little lower down.

'I knew that!' Connie cried over her shoulder, and she flitted across the open pasture, humming to herself.

'Oh, of course! If some people have private information, they can afford to thrust.' This was a snuff-coloured habit into which Miss Sperrit had cannoned down the ride.

'What! Midmore got Sidney to heel? You never did that, Sperrit.' This was Mr Fisher, M.F.H., enlarging the breach Midmore had made.

'No, confound him!' said the father testily. 'Go on, sir! Injecto ter pulvere—you've kicked half the ditch into my eye already.'

They killed that cub a little short of the haven his mother had told him to make for—a two-acre Alsatia of a gorse-patch to which the M.F.H. had been denied access for the last fifteen seasons. He expressed his gratitude before all the field and Mr Sidney, at Mr Sidney's farm-house door.

'And if there should be any poultry claims—' he went on.

'There won't be,' said Midmore. 'It's too like cheating a sucking child, isn't it, Mr Sidney?'

'You've got me!' was all the reply. 'I be used to bein' put upon, but you've got me, Mus' Midmore.'

Midmore pointed to a new brick pig-pound built in strict disregard of the terms of the life-tenant's lease. The gesture told the tale to the few who did not know, and they shouted.

Such pagan delights as these were followed by pagan sloth of evenings when men and women elsewhere are at their brightest. But Midmore preferred to lie out on a yellow silk couch, reading works of a debasing vulgarity; or, by invitation, to dine with the Sperrits and savages of their kidney. These did not expect flights of fancy or phrasing. They lied, except about horses, grudgingly and of necessity, not for art's sake; and, men and women alike, they expressed themselves along their chosen lines with the serene indifference of the larger animals. Then Midmore would go home and identify them, one by one, out of the natural-history books by Mr Surtees, on the table beside the sofa. At first they looked upon him coolly, but when the tale of the removed wire and the recaptured gorse had gone the rounds, they accepted him for a person willing to play their games. True, a faction suspended judgment for a while, because they shot, and hoped that Midmore would serve the glorious mammon of pheasant-raising rather than the unkempt god of fox-hunting. But after he had shown his choice, they did not ask by what intellectual process he had arrived at it. He hunted three, sometimes four, times a week, which necessitated not only one bay gelding (£94:10s.), but a mannerly white-stockinged chestnut (£114), and a black mare, rather long in the back but with a mouth of silk (£150), who so evidently preferred to carry a lady that it would have been cruel to have baulked her. Besides, with that handling she could be sold at a profit. And besides, the hunt was a quiet, intimate, kindly little hunt, not anxious for strangers, of good report in the Field, the servant of one M.F.H., given to hospitality, riding well its own horses, and, with the exception of Midmore, not novices. But as Miss Sperrit observed, after the M.F.H. had said some things to him at a gate: 'It is a pity you don't know as much as your horse, but you will in time. It takes years and yee-ars. I've been at it for fifteen and I'm only just learning. But you've made a decent kick-off.'

So he kicked off in wind and wet and mud, wondering quite sincerely why the bubbling ditches and sucking pastures held him from day to day, or what solace he could find on off days in chasing grooms and brick-layers round outhouses.

To make sure he up-rooted himself one week-end of heavy mid-winter rain, and re-entered his lost world in the character of Galahad fresh from a rest-cure. They all agreed, with an eye over his shoulder for the next comer, that he was a different man; but when they asked him for the symptoms of nervous strain, and led him all through their own, he realized he had lost much of his old skill in lying. His three months' absence, too, had put him hopelessly behind the London field. The movements, the allusions, the slang of the game had changed. The couples had rearranged themselves or were re-crystallizing in fresh triangles, whereby he put his foot in it badly. Only one great soul (he who had written the account of the pig-pound episode) stood untouched by the vast flux of time, and Midmore lent him another fiver for his integrity. A woman took him, in the wet forenoon, to a pronouncement on the Oneness of Impulse in Humanity, which struck him as a polysyllabic resume of Mr Sidney's domestic arrangements, plus a clarion call to 'shock civilization into common-sense'.

'And you'll come to tea with me tomorrow?' she asked, after lunch, nibbling cashew nuts from a saucer. Midmore replied that there were great arrears of work to overtake when a man had been put away for so long.

'But you've come back like a giant refreshed...I hope that Daphne'—this was the lady of the twelve and the eight-page letter—'will be with us too. She has misunderstood herself, like so many of us,' the woman murmured, 'but I think eventually...' she flung out her thin little hands. 'However, these are things that each lonely soul must adjust for itself.'

'Indeed, yes,' said Midmore with a deep sigh. The old tricks were sprouting in the old atmosphere like mushrooms in a dung-pit. He passed into an abrupt reverie, shook his head, as though stung by tumultuous memories, and departed without any ceremony of farewell to—catch a mid-afternoon express where a man meets associates who talk horse, and weather as it affects the horse, all the way down. What worried him most was that he had missed a day with the hounds.

He met Rhoda's keen old eyes without flinching; and the drawing-room looked very comfortable that wet evening at tea. After all, his visit to town had not been wholly a failure. He had burned quite a bushel of letters at his flat. A flat—here he reached mechanically towards the worn volumes near the sofa—a flat was a consuming animal. As for Daphne... He opened at random on the words: 'His lordship then did as desired and disclosed a tableau of considerable strength and variety.' Midmore reflected: 'And I used to think... But she wasn't... We were all babblers and skirters together... I didn't babble much—thank goodness—but I skirted.' He turned the pages backward for more Sortes Surteesianae, and read: 'When at length they rose to go to bed it struck each man as he followed his neighbour upstairs, that the man before him walked very crookedly.' He laughed aloud at the fire.

'What about to-morrow?' Rhoda asked, entering with garments over her shoulder. 'It's never stopped raining since you left. You'll be plastered out of sight an' all in five minutes. You'd better wear your next best, 'adn't you? I'm afraid they've shrank. 'Adn't you best try 'em on?'

'Here?' said Midmore.

"Suit yourself. I bathed you when you wasn't larger than a leg o' lamb,' said the ex-ladies'-maid.

'Rhoda, one of these days I shall get a valet, and a married butler.'

'There's many a true word spoke in jest. But nobody's huntin' tomorrow.'

'Why? Have they cancelled the meet?'

'They say it only means slipping and over-reaching in the mud, and they all 'ad enough of that today. Charlie told me so just now.'

'Oh!' It seemed that the word of Mr Sperrit's confidential clerk had weight.

'Charlie came down to help Mr Sidney lift the gates,' Rhoda continued.

'The floodgates? They are perfectly easy to handle now. I've put in a wheel and a winch.'

'When the brook's really up they must be took clean out on account of the rubbish blockin' 'em. That's why Charlie came down.'

Midmore grunted impatiently. 'Everybody has talked to me about that brook ever since I came here. It's never done anything yet.'

'This 'as been a dry summer. If you care to look now, sir, I'll get you a lantern.'

She paddled out with him into a large wet night. Half-way down the lawn her light was reflected on shallow brown water, pricked through with grass blades at the edges. Beyond that light, the brook was strangling and kicking among hedges and tree-trunks.

'What on earth will happen to the big rose-bed?' was Midmore's first word.

'It generally 'as to be restocked after a flood. Ah!' she raised her lantern. 'There's two garden-seats knockin' against the sun-dial. Now, that won't do the roses any good.'

'This is too absurd. There ought to be some decently thought-out system—for—for dealing with this sort of thing.' He peered into the rushing gloom. There seemed to be no end to the moisture and the racket. In town he had noticed nothing.

'It can't be 'elped,' said Rhoda. 'It's just what it does do once in just so often. We'd better go back.'

All earth under foot was sliding in a thousand liquid noises towards the hoarse brook. Somebody wailed from the house: ''Fraid o' the water! Come 'ere! 'Fraid o' the water!'

'That's Jimmy. Wet always takes 'im that way,' she explained. The idiot charged into them, shaking with terror.

'Brave Jimmy! How brave of Jimmy! Come into the hall. What Jimmy got now?' she crooned.

It was a sodden note which ran: 'Dear Rhoda—Mr Lotten, with whom I rode home this afternoon, told me that if this wet keeps up, he's afraid the fish-pond he built last year, where Coxen's old mill-dam was, will go, as the dam did once before, he says. If it does it's bound to come down the brook. It may be all right, but perhaps you had better look out. C.S.'

'If Coxen's dam goes, that means... I'll 'ave the drawing-room carpet up at once to be on the safe side. The claw-'ammer is in the libery.'

'Wait a minute. Sidney's gates are out, you said?'

'Both. He'll need it if Coxen's pond goes... I've seen it once.'

'I'll just slip down and have a look at Sidney. Light the lantern again, please, Rhoda.'

'You won't get him to stir. He's been there since he was born. But she don't know anything. I'll fetch your waterproof and some top-boots.'

"Fraid o' the water! 'Fraid o' the water!' Jimmy sobbed, pressed against a corner of the hall, his hands to his eyes.

'All right, Jimmy. Jimmy can help play with the carpet,' Rhoda answered, as Midmore went forth into the darkness and the roarings all round. He had never seen such an utterly unregulated state of affairs. There was another lantern reflected on the streaming drive.

'Hi! Rhoda! Did you get my note? I came down to make sure. I thought, afterwards, Jimmy might funk the water!'

'It's me—Miss Sperrit,' Midmore cried. 'Yes, we got it, thanks.'

'You're back, then. Oh, good!... Is it bad down with you?'

'I'm going to Sidney's to have a look.'

'You won't get him out. 'Lucky I met Bob Lotten. I told him he hadn't any business impounding water for his idiotic trout without rebuilding the dam.'

'How far up is it? I've only been there once.'

'Not more than four miles as the water will come. He says he's opened all the sluices.'

She had turned and fallen into step beside him, her hooded head bowed against the thinning rain. As usual she was humming to herself.

'Why on earth did you come out in this weather?' Midmore asked.

'It was worse when you were in town. The rain's taking off

now. If it wasn't for that pond, I wouldn't worry so much. There's Sidney's bell. Come on!' She broke into a run. A cracked bell was jangling feebly down the valley.

'Keep on the road!' Midmore shouted. The ditches were snorting bank-full on either side, and towards the brook-side the fields were afloat and beginning to move in the darkness.

'Catch me going off it! There's his light burning all right.' She halted undistressed at a little rise. 'But the flood's in the orchard. Look!' She swung her lantern to show a front rank of old apple-trees reflected in still, out-lying waters beyond the half-drowned hedge. They could hear above the thud-thud of the gorged floodgates, shrieks in two keys as monotonous as a steam-organ.

'The high one's the pig.' Miss Sperrit laughed.

'All right! I'll get her out. You stay where you are, and I'll see you home afterwards.'

'But the water's only just over the road,' she objected.

'Never mind. Don't you move. Promise?'

'All right. You take my stick, then, and feel for holes in case anything's washed out anywhere. This is a lark!'

Midmore took it, and stepped into the water that moved sluggishly as yet across the farm road which ran to Sidney's front door from the raised and metalled public road. It was half way up to his knees when he knocked. As he looked back Miss Sperrit's lantern seemed to float in mid-ocean.

'You can't come in or the water'll come with you. I've bunged up all the cracks,' Mr Sidney shouted from within. 'Who be ye?'

'Take me out! Take me out!' the woman shrieked, and the pig from his sty behind the house urgently seconded the motion.

'I'm Midmore! Coxen's old mill-dam is likely to go, they say. Come out!'

'I told 'em it would when they made a fish-pond of it. 'Twasn't ever puddled proper. But it's a middlin' wide valley. She's got room to spread... Keep still, or I'll take and duck you in the cellar!... You go 'ome, Mus' Midmore, an' take the law o' Mus' Lotten soon's you've changed your socks.'

'Confound you, aren't you coming out?'

'To catch my death o' cold? I'm all right where I be. I've seen it before. But you can take her. She's no sort o' use or sense... Climb out through the window. Didn't I tell you I'd plugged the door-cracks, you fool's daughter?' The parlour window opened, and the woman flung herself into Midmore's arms, nearly knocking him down. Mr Sidney leaned out of the window, pipe in mouth.

'Take her 'ome,' he said, and added oracularly:

'Two women in one house,
Two cats an' one mouse,
Two dogs an' one bone—
Which I will leave alone.
I've seen it before.' Then he shut and fastened the window.

'A trap! A trap! You had ought to have brought a trap for me. I'll be drowned in this wet,' the woman cried.

'Hold up! You can't be any wetter than you are. Come along!' Midmore did not at all like the feel of the water over his boot-tops.

'Hooray! Come along!' Miss Sperrit's lantern, not fifty yards away, waved cheerily.

The woman threshed towards it like a panic-stricken goose, fell on her knees, was jerked up again by Midmore, and pushed on till she collapsed at Miss Sperrit's feet.

'But you won't get bronchitis if you go straight to Mr Midmore's house,' said the unsympathetic maiden.

'O Gawd! O Gawd! I wish our 'eavenly Father 'ud forgive me my sins an' call me 'ome,' the woman sobbed. 'But I won't go to 'is 'ouse! I won't.'

'All right, then. Stay here. Now, if we run,' Miss Sperrit whispered to Midmore, 'she'll follow us. Not too fast!'

They set off at a considerable trot, and the woman lumbered behind them, bellowing, till they met a third lantern—Rhoda holding Jimmy's hand. She had got the carpet up, she said, and was escorting Jimmy past the water that he dreaded.

'That's all right,' Miss Sperrit pronounced. 'Take Mrs Sidney back with you, Rhoda, and put her to bed. I'll take Jimmy with me. You aren't afraid of the water now, are you, Jimmy?'

'Not afraid of anything now.' Jimmy reached for her hand. 'But get away from the water quick.'

'I'm coming with you,' Midmore interrupted.

'You most certainly are not. You're drenched. She threw you twice. Go home and change. You may have to be out again all night. It's only half-past seven now. I'm perfectly safe.' She flung herself lightly over a stile, and hurried uphill by the foot-path, out of reach of all but the boasts of the flood below.

Rhoda, dead silent, herded Mrs Sidney to the house.

'You'll find your things laid out on the bed,' she said to Midmore as he came up. 'I'll attend to—to this. She's got nothing to cry for.'

Midmore raced into dry kit, and raced uphill to be rewarded by the sight of the lantern just turning into the Sperrits' gate. He came back by way of Sidney's farm, where he saw the light twinkling across three acres of shining water, for the rain had ceased and the clouds were stripping overhead, though the brook was noisier than ever. Now there was only that doubtful mill-pond to look after—that and his swirling world abandoned to himself alone.

'We shall have to sit up for it,' said Rhoda after dinner. And as the drawing-room commanded the best view of the rising flood, they watched it from there for a long time, while all the clocks of the house bore them company.

''Tisn't the water, it's the mud on the skirting-board after it goes down that I mind,' Rhoda whispered. 'The last time Coxen's mill broke, I remember it came up to the second—no, third—step o' Mr Sidney's stairs.'

'What did Sidney do about it?'

'He made a notch on the step. 'E said it was a record. Just like 'im.'

'It's up to the drive now,' said Midmore after another long wait. 'And the rain stopped before eight, you know.'

'Then Coxen's dam 'as broke, and that's the first of the flood-water.' She stared out beside him. The water was rising in sudden pulses—an inch or two at a time, with great sweeps and lagoons and a sudden increase of the brook's proper thunder.

'You can't stand all the time. Take a chair,' Midmore said presently.

Rhoda looked back into the bare room. 'The carpet bein' up does make a difference. Thank you, sir, I will 'ave a set-down.'

'"Right over the drive now,' said Midmore. He opened the window and leaned out. 'Is that wind up the valley, Rhoda?'

'No, that's it! But I've seen it before.'

There was not so much a roar as the purposeful drive of a tide across a jagged reef, which put down every other sound for twenty minutes. A wide sheet of water hurried up to the little terrace on which the house stood, pushed round either corner, rose again and stretched, as it were, yawning beneath the moonlight, joined other sheets waiting for them in unsuspected hollows, and lay out all in one. A puff of wind followed.

'It's right up to the wall now. I can touch it with my finger.' Midmore bent over the window-sill.

'I can 'ear it in the cellars,' said Rhoda dolefully. 'Well, we've done what we can! I think I'll 'ave a look.' She left the room and was absent half an hour or more, during which time he saw a full-grown tree hauling itself across the lawn by its naked roots. Then a hurdle knocked against the wall, caught on an iron foot-scraper just outside, and made a square-headed ripple. The cascade through the cellar-windows diminished.

'It's dropping,' Rhoda cried, as she returned. 'It's only tricklin' into my cellars now.'

'Wait a minute. I believe—I believe I can see the scraper on the edge of the drive just showing!'

In another ten minutes the drive itself roughened and became gravel again, tilting all its water towards the shrubbery.

'The pond's gone past,' Rhoda announced. 'We shall only 'ave the common flood to contend with now. You'd better go to bed.'

'I ought to go down and have another look at Sidney before daylight.'

'No need. You can see 'is light burnin' from all the upstairs windows.'

'By the way. I forgot about her. Where've you put her?'

'In my bed.' Rhoda's tone was ice. 'I wasn't going to undo a room for that stuff.'

'But it—it couldn't be helped,' said Midmore. 'She was half drowned. One mustn't be narrow-minded, Rhoda, even if her position isn't quite—er—regular.'

'Pfff! I wasn't worryin' about that.' She leaned forward to the window. 'There's the edge of the lawn showin' now. It falls as fast as it rises. Dearie'—the change of tone made Midmore jump—'didn't you know that I was 'is first? That's what makes it so hard to bear.' Midmore looked at the long lizard-like back and had no words.

She went on, still talking through the black window-pane:

'Your pore dear auntie was very kind about it. She said she'd make all allowances for one, but no more. Never any more... Then, you didn't know 'oo Charlie was all this time?'

'Your nephew, I always thought.'

'Well, well,' she spoke pityingly. 'Everybody's business being nobody's business, I suppose no one thought to tell you. But Charlie made 'is own way for 'imself from the beginnin'!... But her upstairs, she never produced anything. Just an 'ousekeeper, as you might say. Turned over an' went to sleep straight off. She 'ad the impudence to ask me for 'ot sherry-gruel.'

'Did you give it to her?' said Midmore.

'Me? Your sherry? No!'

The memory of Sidney's outrageous rhyme at the window, and Charlie's long nose (he thought it looked interested at the time) as he passed the copies of Mrs Werf's last four wills, overcame Midmore without warning.

'This damp is givin' you a cold,' said Rhoda, rising. 'There you go again! Sneezin's a sure sign of it. Better go to bed. You can't do any thin' excep''—she stood rigid, with crossed arms—'about me.'

'Well. What about you?' Midmore stuffed the handkerchief into his pocket.

'Now you know about it, what are you goin' to do—sir?'

She had the answer on her lean cheek before the sentence was finished.

'Go and see if you can get us something to eat, Rhoda. And beer.'

'I expec' the larder'll be in a swim,' she replied, 'but old bottled stuff don't take any harm from wet.' She returned with a tray, all in order, and they ate and drank together, and took observations of the falling flood till dawn opened its bleared eyes on the wreck of what had been a fair garden. Midmore, cold and annoyed, found himself humming:

'That flood strewed wrecks upon the grass,

That ebb swept out the flocks to sea.

'There isn't a rose left, Rhoda!

'An awesome ebb and flow it was

To many more than mine and me.

But each will mourn his...

'It'll cost me a hundred.'

'Now we know the worst,' said Rhoda, 'we can go to bed. I'll lay on the kitchen sofa. His light's burnin' still.'

'And she?'

'Dirty old cat! You ought to 'ear 'er snore!'

At ten o'clock in the morning, after a maddening hour in his own garden on the edge of the retreating brook, Midmore went off to confront more damage at Sidney's. The first thing that met him was the pig, snowy white, for the water had washed him out of his new sty, calling on high heaven for breakfast. The front door had been forced open, and the flood had registered its own height in a brown dado on the walls. Midmore chased the pig out and called up the stairs.

'I be abed o' course. Which step 'as she rose to?' Sidney cried from above. 'The fourth? Then it's beat all records. Come up.'

'Are you ill?' Midmore asked as he entered the room. The red eyelids blinked cheerfully. Mr Sidney, beneath a sumptuous patchwork quilt, was smoking.

'Nah! I'm only thankin' God I ain't my own landlord. Take that cheer. What's she done?'

'It hasn't gone down enough for me to make sure.'

'Them floodgates o' yourn'll be middlin' far down the brook by now; an' your rose-garden have gone after 'em. I saved my chickens, though. You'd better get Mus' Sperrit to take the law o' Lotten an' 'is fish-pond.'

'No, thanks. I've trouble enough without that.'

'Hev ye?' Mr Sidney grinned. 'How did ye make out with those two women o' mine last night? I lay they fought.'

'You infernal old scoundrel!' Midmore laughed.

'I be—an' then again I bain't,' was the placid answer. 'But, Rhoda, she wouldn't ha' left me last night. Fire or flood, she wouldn't.'

'Why didn't you ever marry her?' Midmore asked.

'Waste of good money. She was willin' without.'

There was a step on the gritty mud below, and a voice humming. Midmore rose quickly saying: 'Well, I suppose you're all right now.'

'I be. I ain't a landlord, nor I ain't young—nor anxious. Oh, Mus' Midmore! Would it make any odds about her thirty pounds comin' regular if I married her? Charlie said maybe 'twould.'

'Did he?' Midmore turned at the door. 'And what did Jimmy say about it?'

'Jimmy?' Mr Sidney chuckled as the joke took him. 'Oh, he's none o' mine. He's Charlie's look-out.'

Midmore slammed the door and ran downstairs.

'Well, this is a—sweet—mess,' said Miss Sperrit in shortest skirts and heaviest riding-boots. 'I had to come down and have a look at it. "The old mayor climbed the belfry tower." Been up all night nursing your family?'

'Nearly that! Isn't it cheerful?' He pointed through the door to the stairs with small twig-drift on the last three treads.

'It's a record, though,' said she, and hummed to herself:

'That flood strewed wrecks upon the grass, That ebb swept out the flocks to sea.'

'You're always singing that, aren't you?' Midmore said suddenly as she passed into the parlour where slimy chairs had been stranded at all angles.

'Am I? Now I come to think of it I believe I do. They say I always hum when I ride. Have you noticed it?'

'Of course I have. I notice every—'

'Oh,' she went on hurriedly. 'We had it for the village cantata last winter—"The Brides of Enderby."'

'No! "High Tide on the Coast of Lincolnshire." For some reason Midmore spoke sharply.

'Just like that.' She pointed to the befouled walls. 'I say... Let's get this furniture a little straight... You know it too?'

'Every word, since you sang it of course.'

'When?'

'The first night I ever came down. You rode past the drawing-room window in the dark singing it—"And sweeter woman—"'

'I thought the house was empty then. Your aunt always let us use that short cut. Ha—hadn't we better get this out into the passage? It'll all have to come out anyhow. You take the other side.' They began to lift a heavyish table. Their words came jerkily between gasps and their faces were as white as—a newly washed and very hungry pig.

'Look out!' Midmore shouted. His legs were whirled from under him, as the table, grunting madly, careened and knocked the girl out of sight.

The wild boar of Asia could not have cut down a couple more scientifically, but this little pig lacked his ancestor's nerve and fled shrieking over their bodies.

'Are you hurt, darling?' was Midmore's first word, and 'No—I'm only winded—dear,' was Miss Sperrit's, as he lifted her out of her corner, her hat over one eye and her right cheek a smear of mud.

They fed him a little later on some chicken-feed that they found in Sidney's quiet barn, a pail of buttermilk out of the dairy, and a quantity of onions from a shelf in the back-kitchen.

'Seed-onions, most likely,' said Connie. 'You'll hear about this.'

'What does it matter? They ought to have been gilded. We must buy him.'

'And keep him as long as he lives,' she agreed. 'But I think I ought to go home now. You see, when I came out I didn't expect... Did you?'

'No! Yes... It had to come... But if any one had told me an hour ago!... Sidney's unspeakable parlour—and the mud on the carpet.'

'Oh, I say! Is my cheek clean now?'

'Not quite. Lend me your hanky again a minute, darling... What a purler you came!'

'You can't talk. Remember when your chin hit that table and you said "blast"! I was just going to laugh.'

'You didn't laugh when I picked you up. You were going "oo-oo-oo" like a little owl.'

'My dear child—'

'Say that again!'

'My dear child. (Do you really like it? I keep it for my best friends.) My dee-ar child, I thought I was going to be sick there and then. He knocked every ounce of wind out of me—the angel! But I must really go.'

They set off together, very careful not to join hands or take arms.

'Not across the fields,' said Midmore at the stile. 'Come round by—by your own place.'

She flushed indignantly.

'It will be yours in a little time,' he went on, shaken with his own audacity.

'Not so much of your little times, if you please!' She shied like a colt across the road; then instantly, like a colt, her eyes lit with new curiosity as she came in sight of the drive-gates.

'And not quite so much of your airs and graces, Madam,' Midmore returned, 'or I won't let you use our drive as a short cut any more.'

'Oh, I'll be good. I'll be good.' Her voice changed suddenly. 'I swear I'll try to be good, dear. I'm not much of a thing at the best. What made you...'

'I'm worse—worse! Miles and oceans worse. But what does it matter now?'

They halted beside the gate-pillars.

'I see!' she said, looking up the sodden carriage sweep to the front door porch where Rhoda was slapping a wet mat to and fro. 'I see... Now, I really must go home. No! Don't you come. I must speak to Mother first all by myself.'

He watched her up the hill till she was out of sight.

7

THE CITY OF DREADFUL NIGHT

The dense wet heat that hung over the face of land, like a blanket, prevented all hope of sleep in the first instance. The cicalas helped the heat, and the yelling jackals the cicalas. It was impossible to sit still in the dark, empty, echoing house and watch the punkah beat the dead air. So, at ten o'clock of the night, I set my walking-stick on end in the middle of the garden, and waited to see how it would fall. It pointed directly down the moonlit road that leads to the City of Dreadful Night. The sound of its fall disturbed a hare. She limped from her form and ran across to a disused Mahomedan burial-ground, where the jawless skulls and rough-butted shank-bones, heartlessly exposed by the July rains, glimmered like mother o' pearl on the rain-channelled soil. The heated air and the heavy earth had driven the very dead upward for coolness' sake. The hare limped on; snuffed curiously at a fragment of a smoke-stained lamp-shard, and died out, in the shadow of a clump of tamarisk trees.

The mat-weaver's hut under the lee of the Hindu temple was full of sleeping men who lay like sheeted corpses. Overhead blazed the unwinking eye of the Moon. Darkness gives at least a false impression of coolness. It was hard not to believe that the flood of light from above was warm. Not so hot as the Sun, but still sickly warm, and heating the heavy air beyond what was our due. Straight as a bar of polished steel ran the road to the City of Dreadful Night; and on either side of the road lay corpses disposed on beds in fantastic attitudes—one hundred and seventy bodies of men. Some shrouded all in white with bound-up mouths; some naked and black as ebony in the strong light; and one—that lay face upwards with dropped jaw, far away from the others—silvery white and ashen gray.

'A leper asleep; and the remainder wearied coolies, servants, small shopkeepers, and drivers from the hack-stand hard by. The scene—a main approach to Lahore city, and the night a warm one in August.' This was all that there was to be seen; but by no means all that one could see. The witchery of the moonlight was everywhere; and the world was horribly changed. The long line of the naked dead, flanked by the rigid silver statue, was not pleasant to look upon. It was made up of men alone. Were the womenkind, then, forced to sleep in the shelter of the stifling mud-huts as best they might? The fretful wail of a child from a low mud-roof answered the question. Where the children are the mothers must be also to look after them. They need care on these sweltering nights. A black little bullet-head peeped over the coping, and a thin—a painfully thin—brown leg was slid over on to the gutter pipe. There was a sharp clink of glass bracelets; a woman's arm showed for an instant above the parapet, twined itself round the lean little neck, and the child was dragged back, protesting, to the shelter of the bedstead. His thin, high-pitched shriek died out in the thick air almost as soon as it was raised; for even the children of the soil found it too hot to weep.

More corpses; more stretches of moonlit, white road; a string of sleeping camels at rest by the wayside; a vision of scudding jackals; ekka-ponies asleep—the harness still on their backs, and the brass-studded country carts, winking in the moonlight—and again more corpses. Wherever a grain cart atilt, a tree trunk, a sawn log, a couple of bamboos and a few handfuls of thatch cast a shadow, the ground is covered with them. They lie—some face downwards, arms folded, in the dust; some with clasped hands flung up above their heads; some curled up dog-wise; some thrown like limp gunny-bags over the side of the grain carts; and some bowed with their brows on their knees in the full glare of the Moon. It would be a comfort if they were only given to snoring; but they are not, and the likeness to corpses is unbroken in all respects save one. The lean dogs snuff at them and turn away. Here and there a tiny child lies on his father's bedstead, and a protecting arm is thrown round it in every instance. But, for the most part, the children sleep with their mothers on the house-tops. Yellow-skinned white-toothed pariahs are not to be trusted within reach of brown bodies.

A stifling hot blast from the mouth of the Delhi Gate nearly ends my resolution of entering the City of Dreadful Night at this hour. It is a compound of all evil savours, animal and vegetable, that a walled city can brew in a day and a night. The temperature within the motionless groves of plantain and orange-trees outside the city walls seems chilly by comparison. Heaven help all sick persons and young children within the city to-night! The high house-walls are still radiating heat savagely, and from obscure side gullies fetid breezes eddy that ought to poison a buffalo. But the buffaloes do not heed. A drove of them are parading the vacant main street; stopping now and then to lay their ponderous muzzles against the closed shutters of a grain-dealer's shop and to blow thereon like grampuses.

Then silence follows—the silence that is full of the night noises of a great city. A stringed instrument of some kind is just, and only just, audible. High overhead some one throws open a window, and the rattle of the wood-work echoes down the empty street. On one of the roofs a hookah is in full blast; and the men are talking softly as the pipe gutters. A little farther on the noise of conversation is more distinct. A slit of light shows itself between the sliding shutters of a shop. Inside, a stubble-bearded, weary-eyed trader is balancing his account-books among the bales of cotton prints that surround him. Three sheeted figures bear him company, and throw in a remark from time to time. First he makes an entry, then a remark; then passes the back of his hand across his streaming forehead. The heat in the built-in street is fearful. Inside the shops it must be almost unendurable. But the work goes on steadily; entry, guttural growl, and uplifted hand-stroke succeeding each other with the precision of clock-work.

A policeman—turbanless and fast asleep—lies across the road on the way to the Mosque of Wazir Khan. A bar of moonlight falls across the forehead and eyes of the sleeper, but he never stirs. It is close upon midnight, and the heat seems to be increasing. The open square in front of the Mosque is crowded with corpses; and a man must pick his way carefully for fear of treading on them. The moonlight stripes the Mosque's high front of coloured enamel work in broad diagonal bands; and each separate dreaming pigeon in the niches and corners of the masonry throws a squab little shadow. Sheeted ghosts rise up wearily from their pallets, and flit into the dark depths of the building. Is it possible to climb to the top of the great Minars, and thence to look down on the city? At all events the attempt is worth making, and the chances are that the door of the staircase will be unlocked. Unlocked it is; but a deeply sleeping janitor lies across the threshold, face turned to the Moon. A rat dashes out of his turban at the sound of approaching footsteps. The man grunts, opens his eyes for a minute, turns round, and goes to sleep again. All the heat of a decade of fierce Indian summers is stored in the pitch-black, polished walls of the corkscrew staircase. Half-way up, there is something alive, warm, and feathery; and it snores. Driven from step to step as it catches the sound of my advance, it flutters to the top and reveals itself as a yellow-eyed, angry kite. Dozens of kites are asleep on this and the other Minars, and on the domes below. There is the shadow of a cool, or at least a less sultry breeze at this height; and, refreshed thereby, turn to look on the City of Dreadful Night.

Doré might have drawn it! Zola could describe it—this spectacle of sleeping thousands in the moonlight and in the shadow of the Moon. The roof-tops are crammed with men, women, and children; and the air is full of undistinguishable noises. They are restless in the City of Dreadful Night; and small wonder. The marvel is that they can even breathe. If you gaze intently at the multitude you can see that they are almost as uneasy as a daylight crowd; but the tumult is subdued. Everywhere, in the strong light, you can watch the sleepers turning to and fro; shifting their beds and again resettling them. In the pit-like courtyards of the houses there is the same movement.

The pitiless Moon shows it all. Shows, too, the plains outside the city, and here and there a hand's-breadth of the Ravee without the walls. Shows lastly, a splash of glittering silver on a house-top almost directly below the mosque Minar. Some poor soul has risen to throw a jar of water over his fevered body; the tinkle of the falling water strikes faintly on the ear. Two or three other men, in far-off corners of the City of Dreadful Night, follow his example, and the water flashes like heliographic signals. A small cloud passes over the face of the Moon, and the city and its inhabitants—clear drawn in black and white before— fade into masses of black and deeper black. Still the unrestful noise continues, the sigh of a great city overwhelmed with the heat, and of a people seeking in vain for rest. It is only the lower-class women who sleep on the house-tops. What must the torment be in the latticed zenanas, where a few lamps are still twinkling? There are footfalls in the court below. It is the Muezzin—faithful minister; but he ought to have been here an hour ago to tell the Faithful that prayer is better than sleep—the sleep that will not come to the city.

The Muezzin fumbles for a moment with the door of one of the Minars, disappears awhile, and a bull-like roar—a magnificent bass thunder— tells that he has reached the top of the Minar. They must hear the cry to the banks of the shrunken Ravee itself! Even across the courtyard it is almost overpowering. The cloud drifts by and shows him outlined in black against the sky, hands laid upon his ears, and broad chest heaving with the play of his lungs—'Allah ho Akbar'; then a pause while another Muezzin somewhere in the direction of the Golden Temple takes up the call—'Allah ho Akbar'. Again and again; four times in all; and from the bedsteads a dozen men have risen up already—'I bear witness that there is no God but God.' What a splendid cry it is, the proclamation of the creed that brings men out of their beds by scores at midnight! Once again he thunders through the same phrase, shaking with the vehemence of his own voice; and then, far and near, the night air rings with 'Mahomed is the Prophet of God'. It is as though he were flinging his defiance to the far-off horizon, where the summer lightning plays and leaps like a bared sword. Every Muezzin in the city is in full cry, and some men on the roof-tops are beginning to kneel. A long pause precedes the last cry, 'La ilaha Illallah', and the silence closes up on it, as the ram on the head of a cotton-bale.

The Muezzin stumbles down the dark stairway grumbling in his beard. He passes the arch of the entrance and disappears. Then the stifling silence settles down over the City of Dreadful Night. The kites on the Minar sleep again, snoring more loudly, the hot breeze comes up in puffs and lazy eddies, and the Moon slides down towards the horizon. Seated with both elbows on the parapet of the tower, one can watch and wonder over that heat-tortured hive till the dawn. 'How do they live down there? What do they think of? When will they awake?' More tinkling of sluiced water-pots; faint jarring of wooden bedsteads moved into or out of the shadows; uncouth music of stringed instruments softened by distance into a plaintive wail, and one low grumble of far-off thunder. In the courtyard of the mosque the janitor, who lay across the threshold of the Minar when I came up, starts wildly in his sleep, throws his hands above his head, mutters something, and falls back again. Lulled by the snoring of the kites—they snore like over-gorged humans—I drop off into an uneasy doze, conscious that three o'clock has struck, and that there is a slight—a very slight—coolness in the atmosphere. The city is absolutely quiet now, but for some vagrant dog's love-song. Nothing save dead heavy sleep.

Several weeks of darkness pass after this. For the Moon has gone out. The very dogs are still, and I watch for the first light of the dawn before making my way homeward. Again the noise of shuffling feet. The morning call is about to begin, and my night watch is over. 'Allah ho Akbar! Allah ho Akbar!' The east grows gray, and presently saffron; the dawn wind comes up as though the Muezzin had summoned it; and, as one man, the City of Dreadful Night rises from its bed and turns its face towards the dawning day. With return of life comes return of sound. First a low whisper, then a deep bass hum; for it must be remembered that the entire city is on the house-tops. My eyelids weighed down with the arrears of long deferred sleep, I escape from the Minar through the courtyard and out into the square beyond, where the sleepers have risen, stowed away the bedsteads, and are discussing the morning hookah. The minute's freshness of the air has gone, and it is as hot as at first.

'Will the Sahib, out of his kindness, make room?' What is it? Something borne on men's shoulders comes by in the half-light, and I stand back. A woman's corpse going down to the burning-ghat, and a bystander says, 'She died at midnight from the heat.' So the city was of Death as well as Night after all.

8

SWEPT AND GARNISHED

When the first waves of feverish cold stole over Frau Ebermann she very wisely telephoned for the doctor and went to bed. He diagnosed the attack as mild influenza, prescribed the appropriate remedies, and left her to the care of her one servant in her comfortable Berlin flat. Frau Ebermann, beneath the thick coverlet, curled up with what patience she could until the aspirin should begin to act, and Anna should come back from the chemist with the formamint, the ammoniated quinine, the eucalyptus, and the little tin steam-inhaler. Meantime, every bone in her body ached; her head throbbed; her hot, dry hands would not stay the same size for a minute together; and her body, tucked into the smallest possible compass, shrank from the chill of the well-warmed sheets.

Of a sudden she noticed that an imitation-lace cover which should have lain mathematically square with the imitation-marble top of the radiator behind the green plush sofa had slipped away so that one corner hung over the bronze-painted steam pipes. She recalled that she must have rested her poor head against the radiator-top while she was taking off her boots. She tried to get up and set the thing straight, but the radiator at once receded toward the horizon, which, unlike true horizons, slanted diagonally, exactly parallel with the dropped lace edge of the cover. Frau Ebermann groaned through sticky lips and lay still.

'Certainly, I have a temperature,' she said. 'Certainly, I have a grave temperature. I should have been warned by that chill after dinner.'

She resolved to shut her hot-lidded eyes, but opened them in a little while to torture herself with the knowledge of that ungeometrical thing against the far wall. Then she saw a child—an untidy, thin-faced little girl of about ten, who must have strayed in from the adjoining flat. This proved—Frau Ebermann groaned again at the way the world falls to bits when one is sick—proved that Anna had forgotten to shut the outer door of the flat when she went to the chemist. Frau Ebermann had had children of her own, but they were all grown up now, and she had never been a child-lover in any sense. Yet the intruder might be made to serve her scheme of things.

'Make—put,' she muttered thickly, 'that white thing straight on the top of that yellow thing.'

The child paid no attention, but moved about the room, investigating everything that came in her way—the yellow cut-glass handles of the chest of drawers, the stamped bronze hook to hold back the heavy puce curtains, and the mauve enamel, New Art finger-plates on the door. Frau Ebermann watched indignantly.

'Aie! That is bad and rude. Go away!' she cried, though it hurt her to raise her voice. 'Go away by the road you came!' The child passed behind the bed-foot, where she could not see her. 'Shut the door as you go. I will speak to Anna, but—first, put that white thing straight.'

She closed her eyes in misery of body and soul. The outer door clicked, and Anna entered, very penitent that she had stayed so long at the chemist's. But it had been difficult to find the proper type of inhaler, and—

'Where did the child go?' moaned Frau Ebermann—'the child that was here?'

'There was no child,' said startled Anna. 'How should any child come in when I shut the door behind me after I go out? All the keys of the flats are different.'

'No, no! You forgot this time. But my back is aching, and up my legs also. Besides, who knows what it may have fingered and upset? Look and see.'

'Nothing is fingered, nothing is upset,' Anna replied, as she took the inhaler from its paper box.

'Yes, there is. Now I remember all about it. Put—put that white thing, with the open edge—the lace, I mean—quite straight on that—' she pointed. Anna, accustomed to her ways, understood and went to it.

'Now, is it quite straight?' Frau Ebermann demanded.

'Perfectly,' said Anna. 'In fact, in the very centre of the radiator.' Anna measured the equal margins with her knuckle, as she had been told to do when she first took service.

'And my tortoise-shell hair brushes?' Frau Ebermann could not command her dressing-table from where she lay.

'Perfectly straight, side by side in the big tray, and the comb laid across them. Your watch also in the coralline watch-holder. Everything'—she moved round the room to make sure—'everything is as you have it when you are well.' Frau Ebermann sighed with relief. It seemed to her that the room and her head had suddenly grown cooler.

'Good!' said she. 'Now warm my night-gown in the kitchen, so it will be ready when I have perspired. And the towels also. Make the inhaler steam, and put in the eucalyptus; that is good for the larynx. Then sit you in the kitchen, and come when I ring. But, first, my hot-water bottle.'

It was brought and scientifically tucked in.

'What news?' said Frau Ebermann drowsily. She had not been out that day.

'Another victory,' said Anna. 'Many more prisoners and guns.'

Frau Ebermann purred, one might almost say grunted, contentedly.

'That is good too,' she said; and Anna, after lighting the inhaler-lamp, went out.

Frau Ebermann reflected that in an hour or so the aspirin would begin to work, and all would be well. Tomorrow—no, the day after—she would take up life with something to talk over with her friends at coffee. It was rare—every one knew it—that she should be overcome by any ailment. Yet in all her distresses she had not allowed the minutest deviation from daily routine and ritual. She would tell her friends—she ran over their names one by one—exactly what measures she had taken against the lace cover on the radiator-top and in regard to her two tortoise-shell hair brushes and the comb at right angles. How she had set everything in order—everything in order. She roved further afield as she wriggled her toes luxuriously on the hot-water bottle. If it pleased our dear God to take her to Himself, and she was not so young as she had been—there was that plate of the four lower ones in the blue tooth-glass, for instance—He should find all her belongings fit to meet His eye. 'Swept and garnished' were the words that shaped themselves in her intent brain. 'Swept and garnished for—'

No, it was certainly not for the dear Lord that she had swept; she would have her room swept out tomorrow or the day after, and garnished. Her hands began to swell again into huge pillows of nothingness. Then they shrank, and so did her head, to minute dots. It occurred to her that she was waiting for some event, some tremendously important event, to come to pass. She lay with shut eyes for a long time till her head and hands should return to their proper size.

She opened her eyes with a jerk.

'How stupid of me,' she said aloud, 'to set the room in order for a parcel of dirty little children!'

They were there—five of them, two little boys and three

girls—headed by the anxious-eyed ten-year-old whom she had seen before. They must have entered by the outer door, which Anna had neglected to shut behind her when she returned with the inhaler. She counted them backward and forward as one counts scales—one, two, three, four, five.

They took no notice of her, but hung about, first on one foot then on the other, like strayed chickens, the smaller ones holding by the larger. They had the air of utterly wearied passengers in a railway waiting-room, and their clothes were disgracefully dirty.

'Go away!' cried Frau Ebermann at last, after she had struggled, it seemed to her, for years to shape the words.

'You called?' said Anna at the living-room door.

'No,' said her mistress. 'Did you shut the flat door when you came in?'

'Assuredly,' said Anna. 'Besides, it is made to catch shut of itself.'

'Then go away,' said she, very little above a whisper. If Anna pretended not to see the children, she would speak to Anna later on.

'And now,' she said, turning toward them as soon as the door closed. The smallest of the crowd smiled at her, and shook his head before he buried it in his sister's skirts.

'Why—don't—you—go—away?' she whispered earnestly.

Again they took no notice, but, guided by the elder girl, set themselves to climb, boots and all, on to the green plush sofa in front of the radiator. The little boys had to be pushed, as they could not compass the stretch unaided. They settled themselves in a row, with small gasps of relief, and pawed the plush approvingly.

'I ask you—I ask you why do you not go away—why do you not go away?' Frau Ebermann found herself repeating the question twenty times. It seemed to her that everything in the world hung on the answer. 'You know you should not come into houses and rooms unless you are invited. Not houses and bedrooms, you know.'

'No,' a solemn little six-year-old repeated, 'not houses nor bedrooms, nor dining-rooms, nor churches, nor all those places. Shouldn't come in. It's rude.'

'Yes, he said so,' the younger girl put in proudly. 'He said it. He told them only pigs would do that.' The line nodded and dimpled one to another with little explosive giggles, such as children use when they tell deeds of great daring against their elders.

'If you know it is wrong, that makes it much worse,' said Frau Ebermann.

'Oh yes; much worse,' they assented cheerfully, till the smallest boy changed his smile to a baby wail of weariness.

'When will they come for us?' he asked, and the girl at the head of the row hauled him bodily into her square little capable lap.

'He's tired,' she explained. 'He is only four. He only had his first breeches this spring.' They came almost under his armpits, and were held up by broad linen braces, which, his sorrow diverted for the moment, he patted proudly.

'Yes, beautiful, dear,' said both girls.

'Go away!' said Frau Ebermann. 'Go home to your father and mother!'

Their faces grew grave at once.

'H'sh! We can't,' whispered the eldest. 'There isn't anything left.'

'All gone,' a boy echoed, and he puffed through pursed lips. 'Like that, uncle told me. Both cows too.'

'And my own three ducks,' the boy on the girl's lap said sleepily.

'So, you see, we came here.' The elder girl leaned forward a little, caressing the child she rocked.

'I—I don't understand,' said Frau Ebermann 'Are you lost, then? You must tell our police.'

'Oh no; we are only waiting.'

'But what are you waiting for?'

'We are waiting for our people to come for us. They told us to come here and wait for them. So we are waiting till they come,' the eldest girl replied.

'Yes. We are waiting till our people come for us,' said all the others in chorus.

'But,' said Frau Ebermann very patiently—'but now tell me, for I tell you that I am not in the least angry, where do you come from? Where do you come from?'

The five gave the names of two villages of which she had read in the papers.

'That is silly,' said Frau Ebermann. 'The people fired on us, and they were punished. Those places are wiped out, stamped flat.'

'Yes, yes, wiped out, stamped flat. That is why and—I have lost the ribbon off my pigtail,' said the younger girl. She looked behind her over the sofa-back.

'It is not here,' said the elder. 'It was lost before. Don't you remember?'

'Now, if you are lost, you must go and tell our police. They will take care of you and give you food,' said Frau Ebermann. 'Anna will show you the way there.'

'No,'—this was the six-year-old with the smile?—'we must wait here till our people come for us. Mustn't we, sister?'

'Of course. We wait here till our people come for us. All the world knows that,' said the eldest girl.

'Yes.' The boy in her lap had waked again. 'Little children, too—as little as Henri, and he doesn't wear trousers yet. As little as all that.'

'I don't understand,' said Frau Ebermann, shivering. In spite of the heat of the room and the damp breath of the steam-inhaler, the aspirin was not doing its duty.

The girl raised her blue eyes and looked at the woman for an instant.

'You see,' she said, emphasising her statements with her

fingers, 'they told us to wait here till our people came for us. So we came. We wait till our people come for us.'

'That is silly again,' said Frau Ebermann. 'It is no good for you to wait here. Do you know what this place is? You have been to school? It is Berlin, the capital of Germany.'

'Yes, yes,' they all cried; 'Berlin, capital of Germany. We know that. That is why we came.'

'So, you see, it is no good,' she said triumphantly, 'because your people can never come for you here.'

'They told us to come here and wait till our people came for us.' They delivered this as if it were a lesson in school. Then they sat still, their hands orderly folded on their laps, smiling as sweetly as ever.

'Go away! Go away!' Frau Ebermann shrieked.

'You called?' said Anna, entering.

'No. Go away! Go away!'

'Very good, old cat,' said the maid under her breath. 'Next time you may call,' and she returned to her friend in the kitchen.

'I ask you—ask you, please to go away,' Frau Ebermann pleaded. 'Go to my Anna through that door, and she will give you cakes and sweeties. It is not kind of you to come into my room and behave so badly.'

'Where else shall we go now?' the elder girl demanded, turning to her little company. They fell into discussion. One preferred the broad street with trees, another the railway station; but when she suggested an Emperor's palace, they agreed with her.

'We will go then,' she said, and added half apologetically to Frau Ebermann, 'You see, they are so little they like to meet all the others.'

'What others?' said Frau Ebermann.

'The others—hundreds and hundreds and thousands and thousands of the others.'

'That is a lie. There cannot be a hundred even, much less a

thousand,' cried Frau Ebermann.

'So?' said the girl politely.

'Yes. I tell you; and I have very good information. I know how it happened. You should have been more careful. You should not have run out to see the horses and guns passing. That is how it is done when our troops pass through. My son has written me so.'

They had clambered down from the sofa, and gathered round the bed with eager, interested eyes.

'Horses and guns going by—how fine!' some one whispered.

'Yes, yes; believe me, that is how the accidents to the children happen. You must know yourself that it is true. One runs out to look—'

'But I never saw any at all,' a boy cried sorrowfully. 'Only one noise I heard. That was when Aunt Emmeline's house fell down.'

'But listen to me. I am telling you! One runs out to look, because one is little and cannot see well. So one peeps between the man's legs, and then—you know how close those big horses and guns turn the corners—then one's foot slips and one gets run over. That's how it happens. Several times it had happened, but not many times; certainly not a hundred, perhaps not twenty. So, you see, you must be all. Tell me now that you are all that there are, and Anna shall give you the cakes.'

'Thousands,' a boy repeated monotonously. 'Then we all come here to wait till our people come for us.'

'But now we will go away from here. The poor lady is tired,' said the elder girl, plucking his sleeve.

'Oh, you hurt, you hurt!' he cried, and burst into tears.

'What is that for?' said Frau Ebermann. 'To cry in a room where a poor lady is sick is very inconsiderate.'

'Oh, but look, lady!' said the elder girl.

Frau Ebermann looked and saw.

'Au revoir, lady.' They made their little smiling bows and curtseys undisturbed by her loud cries. 'Au revoir, lady. We will wait till our people come for us.'

When Anna at last ran in, she found her mistress on her knees, busily cleaning the floor with the lace cover from the radiator, because, she explained, it was all spotted with the blood of five children—she was perfectly certain there could not be more than five in the whole world—who had gone away for the moment, but were now waiting round the corner, and Anna was to find them and give them cakes to stop the bleeding, while her mistress swept and garnished that Our dear Lord when He came might find everything as it should be.

ABOUT TERRY O'BRIEN

Terry O'Brien is an academic with three decades of experience in teaching language and communication skills in India and abroad. He also headed a college under the auspices of the University of Delhi.

A prolific writer, with several books to his credit, Terry O'Brien is a reputed professional motivational speaker and a quizmaster.